The Long White

The Iowa Short Fiction Award

Prize money for the award is provided by

a grant from the Iowa Arts Council

The Long White

SHARON DILWORTH

UNIVERSITY OF IOWA PRESS

IOWA CITY

University of Iowa Press, Iowa City 52242
Copyright © 1988 by Sharon Dilworth
All rights reserved
Printed in the United States of America
First edition, 1988

Typesetting by G & S Typesetters, Austin, Texas
Printing and binding by Malloy Lithographing, Ann Arbor, Michigan

The publication of this book is supported by a grant from the National
Endowment for the Arts in Washington, D.C., a federal agency.

Some of these stories have previously appeared, in a slightly altered form, in the
North American Review, Indiana Review, and *Michigan Quarterly Review.*

Library of Congress Cataloging-in-Publication Data

Dilworth, Sharon.
The long white/Sharon Dilworth.— 1st ed.
p.   cm.—(The Iowa short fiction award)
Contents: Winter mines—Mad Dog Queen—Miles from Coconut Grove—The
Seeney stretch—Lunch at Archibald's—The lady on the plane—Independence
Day—Lip service résumé—The long white.
ISBN 0-87745-216-4
I. Title. II. Series.
PS3554.I436L6   1988
813'.54—dc19   88-17307
                             CIP

For

Charlie Baxter

and

Maxine Rodburg

Contents

Winter Mines

Everyone's heard by now that Barbara Wyatt swallowed a half can of Drano. My husband says, in this town, news like that doesn't need any help getting around—people just want to talk about it. Nancy Whitney was in the supermarket on Third Street this morning and she told me she heard Barbara did it in front of a full-length mirror. They found her on the bathroom hamper where she had ripped off her sweater and torn her blouse trying to release the burning pain in her stomach. By the time they got her to the hospital, her lips, which had touched the can, had swollen black.

Nancy was sweating in her down jacket in the supermarket. She rubbed her pregnant belly in circular motions.

"I knew Barbara was depressed," she said. "But I didn't see anything like this coming. I don't think there was any warning at all."

"I didn't talk to her that much," I said. "Not since she moved back to town."

"It's the winter," Nancy said. "I know it's the winter. Fifty-seven inches of snow fell last month alone. And the winds have been coming off the lake at such high speeds that everyone's having trouble just standing up."

Nancy and I tried to hug good-bye, but her eight-month pregnancy wouldn't let us get very close. She went to stand in the ten-item-or-less line with the bag of birdseed and a gallon of milk and I pushed my grocery cart to the household supply aisle. I picked up a can of Drano. The red cap is fastened so tightly that a knife is needed to break the seal. On one side of the can a skull is sketched next to a poison warning: "Contains sodium hydroxide (caustic lye) corrosive. May cause blindness. Always keep out of reach of children. Store on high shelf or in locked cabinet. Harmful or fatal if swallowed."

I wondered how much of the can Barbara had swallowed and I wondered if she knew how much it was going to hurt. Had there been a moment when she wanted to stop what she had done?

My husband doesn't want to hear about Barbara Wyatt. He can't think about anything depressing.

"Please," he asked me this morning. "Don't talk about her in front of me. I don't see why you keep talking about her."

"Barbara was a friend of mine," I said. "I want to talk about her."

"All right. But not with me. Not right now. I can't listen to other people's problems," he said. He brought a roll of paper towels to the kitchen table and folded two separate sheets in half and then again so the coffee mugs wouldn't mark the wood table. He spent yesterday afternoon scrubbing the table with toothpaste trying to get the ring marks out of the wood. I can still smell the mint.

"I don't have time to get involved with everyone else's problems," he said.

"I'm not asking you to get involved with anything, I just want you to listen to me."

"Let's talk about normal things. Nothing depressing," he said. He drank his coffee in long swallows.

"It shouldn't affect you."

"I don't want to talk about someone's suicide."

"But you don't talk to me about anything else," I said. "Everything depresses you."

"A lot of bad things have happened this year," he said. He spooned some jelly on his toast and spread it out evenly with his knife.

"What? What bad things have happened to you?" I asked. I got up from the table and dumped the rest of my coffee down the sink. He refuses to keep coffee with caffeine in the house. He says it aggravates him, but I can't get used to the taste of coffee with nothing in it.

"I'm not going to fight with you," he said.

"Nothing in your life has changed." I repeated the same thing I've said to him since Christmas. "Your life is exactly the same as it is every winter."

"Don't be ignorant." He got up from the table and left the kitchen, leaving the toast on the plate.

"What's so different about your life right now?" I called.

"I won't fight with you," he shouted. I could hear him walking around the living room.

"We're not fighting. I just want you to talk with me."

He didn't answer, but I continued. "You're making everything up in your mind. You're the one that's making yourself depressed. Nothing's happened. Nothing's changed."

When we fight, he shuts up. He won't argue with me. He says it's just a waste of time, because I refuse to look at things the same way he does. In the mornings he makes a list of what has to be done around the house. He spends every weekend scrubbing with bleach and ammonia. During the week he works on projects he finds for himself, like mending holes in the summer screens or rearranging the boxes of junk in the spare bedroom.

Even though he won't answer me, I know I'm right. Nothing has changed. The mines closed the same time they do every year, the week before Thanksgiving. There's a lot of talk about the mines not reopening, but that goes on every year. I don't think it's any worse than it was last year. Someone said something to my husband and he's convinced that the mines are closed forever. He's acting like he doesn't have a job. During Christmas vacation he decided not to leave the house. He says when he goes out he runs into people, like the bartender at the Third Base Bar, who ask him what he thinks about the mines. Last time he went out the guys at the liquor store bet him fifty dollars that the mines would stay shut once the snow melts. My husband says it's too hopeless to talk about.

The woman at the checkout counter asks me if I was a friend of Barbara's.

"In grade school," I tell her. "We were real good friends in grade school."

"I thought I remembered you two coming in here." The woman sits back on a stool she has behind the counter and shakes her head. Her sweater is buttoned up around the neck and she wears brown driving gloves to punch the cash register keys. The front door of the store automatically opens and closes, letting the wind in. I button my coat.

"That was a lot of years ago," she says without looking at my groceries. "Didn't she leave town for a while? I remember something about her getting a job somewhere else."

"She just moved back here." I pick up a newspaper for my husband. It is the newspaper from downstate which never writes about what's going on in the Upper Peninsula. It's the only newspaper he'll read.

"I feel so sorry for her family," the woman says. "What they must be thinking right now. It really makes you wonder."

I don't remember the woman changing over the years. I've been going to the store every day and she has always looked the same to me. Her gray hair frames her face and her glasses hang around her neck on a long black cord.

"It's just her father," I tell her. I open a brown bag and hold the box of spaghetti so the woman can see the price. She rings it on the machine and pushes the other groceries slowly down the rubber mat.

Barbara lived across the street from me when we were in grade school. We were exactly the same age. She didn't have a mother and her father let me sleep over every weekend night. My mother thought two nights in a row was too much, but she let me do it because she felt sorry for Barbara, being without a mother. Barbara and I would listen to her father's Harry Nilsson albums and would drink Coca-Cola out of wine glasses filled with ice cubes. She knew the words to the songs on all his records by heart and I would read them off the back of the album cover to sing along with her. Barbara loved to bake things—anything with sugar in it. One time we stayed up all night, waiting for a cake to cool so we could frost it with caramel frosting that Barbara had made by melting a bag of old Halloween caramels. I remember the only time she talked about not having a mother.

"My father would love to find a new mother for me," she said. "But I don't want one."

"Maybe he's looking for a mother for himself," I said. I had overheard my mother telling someone that Barbara's father was out to get a new wife.

"No," she said. "He doesn't care about things like that. He worries about me. He can take care of me, but he won't. He thinks I should be a part of a family."

"But don't you want to have a mother?"

"Not really. I don't need one," Barbara said. "I'd like to have a mother for only one reason. If I had a mother then she could braid my hair. I'd grow my hair as long as yours is."

My hair in grade school was long and straight. It was thin and wouldn't hold a curl even if I slept in curlers all night. I usually wore it braided on the sides and tied the ends with kitchen rubber bands that snagged and knotted when I pulled them out to wash my hair.

"It's not so great having long hair," I said. "You have to spend a lot of time washing it. My mom makes me come straight home from school to wash it at four o'clock so it will be dry by the time I go to bed."

"But my father won't even let me have long hair. He says it's too much trouble and he doesn't know how to take care of it."

"I braid my own hair now," I said. "My mother just yells about my hair. She says she finds it all over the house."

"At least you know how to braid it. I don't even know how to do that. I never learned."

"I can teach you. You just have to practice getting the rubber bands in without knotting your hair."

We pulled strands of yarn out of an afghan Barbara was making for a Christmas gift. I showed her how to braid the thick pieces into one strand. I showed her how to turn the right section over the left and then start to intertwine the middle section. She practiced on the yarn, then I untied my own hair and she braided a straight plait down my back. I had to put the rubber bands on the end.

I walk home down the center of the street, hugging the bag of groceries in both arms. The muscles above my elbows ache and I shift the weight of the bag down my arms, but it doesn't relieve the pressure. The streets are empty. I keep my head tucked into the collar of my jacket listening for the sound of a car. When I get home, my husband is sitting on the couch, not doing anything.

"Cold out?" he asks.

"It's freezing."

"You shouldn't go out so much. We have enough to eat right here. You're going to get sick if you keep going out in this weather."

"I thought you were going to get someone to help you jump-start the car." I rest the bag of groceries on the coffee table, while I take off my boots. The snow melts quickly, wetting the carpet. "I'd like to have at least one car running by the weekend."

"Why do you need a car this week?"

"It'd be nice to have one to run some errands. I don't like to go out at night without a car." His car is sitting in the driveway, out of gas. He says he doesn't need one, but last week my car died just as I was turning the corner of our block. Two kids from the junior high helped me push it in front of the house and it's been there ever since.

He won't talk about it. "Anything new happening out there?"

"Not much." I give him the newspaper. He tucks a corner of it under his leg without looking at it, which bothers me. I wanted him to read it. I take my boots into the bedroom, where I have compositions to correct. The principal at the school doesn't like us to use the public library because there might be students around. During the spring break, when the high school is closed, I set up a desk in the bedroom. It's really a card table with a dining room chair pulled up to it and one of the lamps brought in from the living room. I work for a half an hour before my husband comes in and sits on the edge of the bed. He watches me correct the papers.

"Do you want me to help?"

"No. That's okay."

"I did compositions in high school. I know what teachers look for in them. Read them aloud. I'll tell you what grade I would give them."

The high school counselor talked to a group of miners' wives in January. She told us how important it is to have patience. She said the worst thing you can do is to argue all the time.

"You'll get bored," I tell him. "It's not a very interesting topic."

"Do you have any football players in this class?" he asks.

"Two."

"Read those first."

"That's not fair, if you know they're guys," I say. But I always look at the name at the top of the composition before I read or grade the paper. "Besides, you don't want to hear compositions. They're just as boring as they were when you were in high school. Why don't you go down to Vinnie's? I saw some of the guys down there."

"I know what they're talking about," he says. "It'll be boring to be with them."

"I think they're watching the hockey game."

"But they're talking about the same things. I can hear their conversation from here."

"You don't know that." I stop pretending to read the paper in front of me.

"Can't you hear it? The whole town is buzzing. Drano and closing. Don't you listen when you go out? Can't you hear what everyone's saying?"

"It's not true. The town is not that small."

"Bullshit."

Without noticing, I have been writing on my hand with the red marker—tiny lines across my knuckles when I thought the cap was on.

"You know what I was thinking this morning?" my husband asks me. "I was wondering if all the color around the mines would fade."

"Color?" I am thinking about my hands and the pen marks. My husband is looking at my fingers too. But I know what he is talking about. The iron ore produces red particles which float in the air around the mines. The particles land on flat surfaces and dye them light pink. All the houses in the area are light pink—even the whitewall tires of the cars. My husband tells me the old guys who work at the security gate have pink teeth.

"No one said the mines are closing," I tell him. "You're just making that up. You're driving yourself crazy."

"Do you think I should call Lansing?" My husband stretches out on the bed. He pushes the pillow on the floor with his feet and stares up at the ceiling. He doesn't need sleep. He slept the whole month of January. He reminded me of a black bear. But not now. He has lost so much weight that his face has changed. His skin is tight across his cheek bones. He told me how much he weighs and it is just three pounds more than I weigh.

"Why would you call Lansing?"

"I want to talk to the governor about the mines. I have a right to know if I still have a job."

"No one's going to tell you anything you don't already know," I say.

"The mines are supposed to open on April 1. If they're not going to open, I have a right to know that now so I can start doing something about it." He talks to me with his eyes closed, his body flat on the bed.

"Last year you didn't start until April 14 and you were just as nervous about starting."

"There was a snowstorm. We couldn't work till then."

"You worry like this every year. The mines always open even after a winter of everyone believing that they won't."

His breathing has changed and I can tell he's sleeping. I stare at the papers in front of me, but the words disappear as I focus on the green petal of the flower in the bedspread. Someone told me that the ambulance driver thought Barbara had cut herself on glass, there had been so much blood. But the blood didn't have anything to do with the Drano. It was from her earlobe. She had pulled a tiny gold earring straight through her skin. They think it got caught in her sweater when she ripped it off her body.

I leave the compositions spread on the card table. I will do them later when he is not in the room. It makes me feel guilty to have things to do when he is around. I take my coffee mug from the drain board and bring it to the basement steps where there's a new jug of wine. I keep a gallon of rosé on the last step. My husband thinks it is the same bottle sitting there since Christmas but I have replaced it twice. I drink a glass of wine at dinner in front of him, but I want to have more. I think I could drink a whole bottle of wine and not feel anything. I sit on the bottom step, listening to the sounds of my house. Through my sweater I can feel the cold steel rim where the next step hits my back.

My husband and I argued the night before about money. He is getting nervous about spending money on food. He wants to start freezing meat so we will have something to eat in the summer months. He said it upsets him to see me spending so much money on groceries.

"We should start living on your salary," he told me last night.

"What about your unemployment check?" I asked him. "You're still collecting unemployment. You're getting your money every two weeks."

"I'm not going to cash those anymore. I'm going to open up another savings account."

"Why? We have enough money."

"Now. But we don't know about the future."

"You don't know that the mines are going to stay closed," I said. "You're just getting paranoid. Don't they always threaten to close?"

"To strike. Not to close. This is the first year they've really threatened to close for good," he said. "I just want to prepare for it."

"I remember last year. You were worried then that they were going to shut down. I remember because you started reading the classifieds in the Detroit newspaper. You told me you were thinking about moving downstate last year."

"This year I can feel it. Everyone's out of work this year. If I lose my job, we are going to move. I won't find anything here in town."

"How come you're the only guy in town who's dead sure they're closing?" I asked.

"I wish you could see things the same way I do," he said. And then he shut up. He refused to say anything else.

I fill the coffee mug again. The wine is bitter at first taste, but smooth as I drink more. I drink two refills and go upstairs when I hear my husband moving around. I have a head rush from drinking so fast. The sun's late shadows fall across the kitchen table to my ski jacket hanging on the back of the chair. My husband is in the bathroom. I can hear the pipes in the walls moan as he turns the faucets on and off. He has started taking long showers, sometimes up to an hour. Afterward his fingertips are wrinkled and swollen to a soft pink. He says they hurt because they are so tender. I don't want to be in the house anymore. I am tired of the day, the same as it was yesterday.

Nancy is surprised when she opens the door. "I'm so glad you stopped by."

"I was just up at the drugstore and thought you might want a little company," I say.

"You're getting stir crazy too?" she guesses. She smiles and tugs at the end of her shirt, which rides up over her belly. "If I watch any more afternoon television, I'll kill myself." Her voice trails off.

I turn to the door, but she has already seen that I am crying. I cover my face with my hands to hide the tears. I can't keep quiet.

"Please don't," she says. "It was stupid of me. I wasn't thinking."

I shake my head and try to swallow so I can speak, but there is too much in the way. I want to leave without saying anything else. Nancy takes my hands away from my face and holds them in her own.

She stands in front of me, rubbing my fingers, which are so numb I can barely feel her warmth. I catch my breath. "I'm sorry."

"I said it without thinking," Nancy says. "Please forget it." Her arms are swollen. The elastic arm bands of her shirt are too tight and there are red lines in the skin above her wrists.

We go into the kitchen and Nancy pours two cups of tea. She sits down and lights a cigarette. "I know I'm too far along to be smoking," she says. "I found a pack under the cushions in the couch. I just smoked a couple this afternoon."

I sip the hot drink and swallow the last of the tears in my throat. The overhead light fills the room with false brightness. I know I am overreacting because of the wine, but I feel calmer listening to Nancy.

"My mother always told me not to get pregnant in the winter. She said nothing could drive you crazier."

"Is Bob away?" My voice is thick. I cough, trying to clear it.

"Till Thursday."

Nancy's husband drives a truck for a beer distributor. He drives down to Chicago for the pickup and then into Milwaukee for the first delivery. He goes northwest for stops near Green Bay and then north into the Upper Peninsula. It takes him three days to make the deliveries.

"Does it bother you when he's away so much?" I ask. My throat is raspy and my head heavy from crying.

"Sometimes I'm afraid I'll have the baby when he's on the road," Nancy says. She taps the side of her cup with manicured nails. "He's going to take some time off when I'm due, but I don't know about that. I'm worried about having him around all day waiting. He'll probably make me so nervous that I'll never have this baby."

"No. You'll be fine."

"How's your husband?" Nancy asks. "I heard the winter's not treating him so good this year."

"Who told you that?" I ask. My heart quickens. "Where did you hear that?"

"You know how it is." Nancy looks away from me. "He really won't leave the house?"

I stare down at my half-filled cup. I didn't know anyone knew about my husband. It makes him sound weak, as if he doesn't have the same strength the others have. I feel guilty that I can't confide in Nancy, but I don't want to talk about him.

"It's a bad winter all around," Nancy says. Her voice is smooth. She sounds neither surprised nor upset, but accepting. "Barbara's death really scared me. She was always such a quiet person. Remember how quiet she was?"

"Not really," I say. "She talked all the time."

"Maybe she was just shy."

I don't know if I am telling the truth, but I continue to argue with Nancy. "I don't know why you said that. Barbara was normal. She was just like everyone else."

"I didn't say she was different," Nancy says. Her skin is transparent under her eyes—I can see the dark veins right underneath her skin. She looks tired.

"Everyone wants to make Barbara out to be weird. She wasn't. She was just like everyone else." I feel strong with my words and my voice gets louder. "The only difference between Barbara and everyone else is that Barbara didn't have a mother."

"What?"

"Barbara didn't have a mother."

Nancy watches me drink the last of my tea. When I finish, I get up and put my coat back on. I lean over and kiss Nancy on the cheek, where the skin is swollen. "I'll stop by and see how you're doing next week. I promise. Have you thought about what you're going to name the baby?"

"I have some names in mind, but nothing for sure." Nancy doesn't get up from the chair.

Already at eight o'clock the streets are quiet. The inside lights of the houses are enclosed by the frost in the windows. Hidden, everyone is protected from the night. As I turn the corner on Third Street, the wind pushes me forward and I stop to keep my balance. Ahead, Lake Superior is a black hole in the darkness surrounding me. I see the untwining of a braid of hair, the right piece loosening from the left and the middle strand unwinding, letting it hang free.

Mad Dog Queen

The bathwater was already cold. Jim flipped the soap with his toe, trying to decide whether to get out or refill the tub, when Beth walked in and told him he had to hitchhike up to L'Anse with her on Friday. It was winter carnival up there, she explained, and this would be her third title. She had been crowned L'Anse's Mad Dog Queen two years in a row. The contest was simple—nothing to do with beauty or talent. The winner was the first woman to down a quart of Mad Dog 20-20 wine. There were two prizes: a ride through town on the winter carnival float alongside the Jack Daniels King and a check for three hundred dollars.

"A drinking contest?" Jim asked. He took the washcloth and covered himself with it, but Beth wasn't looking at him anyway. "Why would you go all the way up there for a drinking contest?"

"I win," Beth said. "I always win." She sat on the edge of the sink, her hip pressed up against the mirror as if knowing he would say yes right away. He usually did anything she wanted him to.

"Doesn't it make you sick to drink all that wine?" Jim asked. He watched her, looking at herself in the steamy mirror. He thought she was beautiful. Where most of the other girls wore their hair long and knotted in ponytails, Beth kept hers short. She said it was New York style. Now, wet from the snow, it hung on her forehead like black string. She combed through it with her fingers.

"I don't swallow," she said. "I open my throat and pour it all down at once." She threw back her head and pointed to the base of her neck, where the skin was still pink from the wind. "You have to keep this part open."

"It sounds kind of disgusting," Jim said. His fingers were soft from the bathwater, numb and wrinkled at the tips. "I can't imagine a bunch of women sitting in a bar slugging down bottles of wine."

"It's only a quart," Beth said. She got up and for a minute

19

Jim thought she was coming over to him. Instead she went to the toilet and pulled some paper off the roll. She blew her nose loudly.

"You have to go with me, Jim. I can't hitch alone."

"Was I your first choice?" Jim asked.

"If I say yes, will you go?" She threw the toilet paper in the trash and reached for her mittens.

"First tell me the truth," Jim said. He let the washcloth float around his feet.

"Okay," she said. "I haven't asked anyone else."

And, totally infatuated with her, Jim said he'd go.

Their first ride out of Marquette got them to Koski Korners at eight-thirty, only two miles from where they'd started. Beth was furious. Her dark eyes glared at Jim in the few rare moments she looked at him. Angry at the late start, the cold, the short first ride, she was also mad at Jim for agreeing with Birdie, the gas station attendant, that they should wait inside instead of on the highway.

"The contest starts at midnight," Beth said. She stood in front of the door with a two-pound bag of cheese popcorn and a fistful of beef jerky. These were her supplies to build up thirst. She wouldn't drink anything, not even water, before the contest. "I'd feel better if we were on the side of the road."

"You plan to walk all the way there?" Jim asked.

"No. I plan to get a ride," she said.

"It's freezing out," Jim said. He pushed their backpack against the frosted glass and crouched down near the space heater. The gas station smelled of rusty fuel and onions, the kind from inside a submarine sandwich. Birdie offered them a beer. His large hands waved to the six-pack on the counter. He had lowered the sound of the portable television set hidden next to the cash register, which was tuned to a show about dressing venison.

"They're not going to wait for me," Beth said. "I mean no

one's sitting up in the bar taking attendance. They'll yell 'on your mark, get set, go' and I'll still be a hundred miles away yakking away with you."

"Is that how those contests begin?" Jim asked. He got up and took the beer, pulling his sweater down over his hand before touching the bottle. "On your mark, get set, go?"

"Anyone going up to the Keweenaw'll stop in here," Birdie said. He smiled, his teeth overflowing in his mouth as if his jaw had been broken more than once. "Skytta's Standard closes down at six. We're the last place open till you get up near L'Anse."

"You don't hitchhike from inside a gas station," Beth said. She glanced quickly at Birdie and then turned her back to the counter. "I've never heard of anything so stupid."

"We'll die out on the highway," Jim said. "Let's at least get warm before we go out again."

Jim rarely argued with Beth. She was not the kind of person who would tolerate being wrong. She did things her way and, if people didn't agree, she did them alone. Jim tried to change certain things about her, especially the idea that she wanted him as a friend and nothing more. They slept together only when she had too much to drink. She would wake up on those mornings and tell him she didn't remember doing it. Her boyfriends, the guys she did remember doing it with, had to be from the Lower Peninsula. She wanted to meet guys from Detroit, Flint, anywhere south of Saginaw—the big cities where the guys smelled of machines and soap. Jim was from Escanaba, a small city more than triple the size of her home-town L'Anse, but not far south enough to guarantee her a way out of the Upper Peninsula. Jim had accused her of only going out with guys to find a magic carpet ride across the Mackinac Bridge and she had agreed. "That's exactly what I want," she had said. "Some sort of way out of here." He offered to take her anywhere. "You don't mean it," she said. But he did mean it.

Beth moved stiffly around the small cleared area in front of the coolers. Underneath her jacket she wore two sweat shirts. The green hood of one was bunched up around her neck and she tugged at it, stretching the material so it hung without shape.

"Let's just try the road," Beth said. "If it gets too bad, we'll come back in."

Jim sipped his beer, thinking of ways to stall her. "This here's the reigning winter carnival queen." He introduced Beth to Birdie.

"The Mad Dog Queen?" Birdie asked. "Is that contest tonight?"

Beth wiped the window with a mittened hand and pressed her face up to the glass. She ignored Birdie's question, the same way she ignored Jim. The oversized bag of popcorn was tucked under her arm like a pillow.

"So that's why you're so nutty to get up to L'Anse," Birdie said. The folds of his stomach overlapped as he laughed.

"This is her third year," Jim said. "We've got to make it up there by midnight."

"You've got plenty of time," Birdie said. He pointed to the clock hanging between the windows covered with newspaper comics to block the wind. The clock, an advertisement for the National Ski Hall of Fame in Michigamme, had a downhill racer in the center. His stocking cap stuck straight up, forming the number 1 in the 12.

"Not that much time," Beth said.

"I bet you're a winner," Birdie said. He got up from the stool and leaned over the counter closer to Beth. "You Indians sure can drink."

"What makes you think I'm an Indian?" Beth asked.

"Never heard of a Mad Dog Queen that wasn't one."

"Well, maybe you're wrong about this one," she said. Jim watched her pull her hat down and knew she was covering the black hair on her forehead.

"I don't think so," Birdie said. He winked over at Jim. "I can tell an Indian a mile away. You all got those eyes. Dark as can be. Every single one of you."

"You should talk about us drinking," Beth said. "You're a Finn. Everyone knows they're alcoholics."

She pushed open the door and a sharp blast of cold air ran in. Jim stood up and grabbed the backpack by the strap.

"They got tempers too," Birdie said. He offered Jim another beer for the road.

The ride up was slow and quiet. The driver didn't say much. He sat hunched over the steering wheel close to the cleared square on the windshield. The rest of the truck was iced up, making it impossible to see out of the dark interior. The dash lights glowed, illuminating the man's hands wrapped around the wheel, his knuckles the color of iron ore. Beth ate through the popcorn bag, wiping the cheese off her hands down the front of her jeans. Jim could feel her hipbone knocking into his where the seat sagged between them. The radio tuned out, leaving only static.

"Your breath is foul," Jim whispered in her ear.

"Wait till I finish these," Beth said. She rattled the packages of beef jerky. "Give me a sip of your beer."

"No. You're in training."

"Just a sip," she said. "All I can taste is salt." She leaned over and licked his neck. "Even on you."

She was always doing things like that. Tonight she would probably get drunk and they would sleep together. On Monday things would be back to normal. She would probably come to his room and start talking about a guy she wanted to go out with from Kalamazoo, never mentioning what happened over the weekend. He just couldn't help himself when she was around. Jim let his mind wander until he could see the straight line of her back, the sharp V of her shoulder blades, the color of her skin so much darker than his. He circled two holes in the side window at eye level and stared out at the continuous line of evergreens bordering the highway.

"Remember about Leena," Beth said. "If she's home, you can just ignore her."

Jim nodded, forgetting she couldn't see him.

"You know what I'm talking about?" she asked.

"Sure. I remember," he said.

Beth had told him about her father's girlfriend Leena more than once. Whenever Jim brought her up, Beth waved the question away. "She's not important," she would say. "She doesn't mean anything to anyone." Beth had told him that Leena moved into the house a year before her mother moved out. Both her parents wanted the divorce, but neither could afford to live anywhere else. That winter her mother had slept on the pull-out couch in the living room; in the spring Leena and her father moved a bed into the room over the garage.

Jim knew about the fights between Leena and Beth's mother. Her mother had been yelling at Leena one day and Leena had turned around and thrown soup down the front of her mother's chest. When Jim asked if her mother had been hurt, Beth told him the soup hadn't been hot.

"His girlfriend can't cook," Beth said. "She only goes into the kitchen when she wants to open the refrigerator door. That soup had probably been sitting on the stove for days."

Jim knew that Beth was afraid of having Leena in the house with her two brothers. "It's bad," Beth told Jim one night. "They're not even sixteen yet."

When Jim pressed her on it, she let him know only a little more. "No one talks about it. They ignore it. Especially my mother," Beth said. "If she knows what's going on, she doesn't do anything."

They took the ride all the way into town to the IGA store and then walked up the hill to Beth's house. The snow was knee deep and Jim had a hard time keeping up with her.

"Leena's going to ask you a million questions," Beth said. She waited for him in front of the house. "Don't tell her anything. If she wants to know something, she'll worm it out of you anyway." Beth knocked once before letting herself in. She turned to him in the dark hallway. "We don't have to stay here. I asked my brothers to help find us someplace to sleep."

Leena was lying on the couch in front of the television set. She glanced up quickly when Beth walked in.

"Where's Dad?" Beth asked.

"Working."

"Where?"

"He's doing snow removal."

"Around here?"

"Maybe if you called once in a while you'd know these things." Leena pushed the white blanket off her legs and turned to face Beth. "That way you wouldn't have to drill me every time you came home."

Beth walked out of the room and slammed a door in the back of the house. Jim stood in the front entrance, making a big deal of wiping his boots on the small rug.

"Who's your friend?" Leena called to Beth. "Does he have a name?"

"Jim." He stepped through the archway, deciding his boots were dry enough to walk on the uncovered floors. The room was practically bare. Besides the couch and the television, there was no other furniture in the room. The one lamp was set on the floor, most of the light coming from an overhead fixture in the kitchen.

"You can sit down if you want," Leena said. She was younger than Jim had expected. Her blonde hair was pulled up in a high ponytail at the back of her head and her skin was pale, typical of the Finns from around L'Anse. "I'm Leena."

Jim nodded. She wore a man's button-down shirt, the tails tied in a knot below her hips. She was big, almost heavy enough to call fat.

"Did Beth tell you about me?" she asked.

"No," Jim lied. "Not really."

"She didn't tell you she hates me?" Leena asked. She put her feet down on the floor, pushing herself forward to the edge of the couch. Her face was puffy, as if they had caught her sleeping.

"No," Jim said. Leena smirked and he wondered if she had expected him to say yes.

"She can't stand me," Leena said. She patted the cushion next to her. "Sit down."

"I think we're leaving right away," he said.

"Is she in town for the chugging contest?"

"Yes," he said. "It starts at midnight."

"She's only doing it for the money." Leena got up from the couch with a cigarette in her mouth and came over to Jim. She handed him the blue plastic lighter and cocked her head to one side, waiting for him to light it for her.

"You'd think if you could smoke those things, you could at least light them for yourself," Beth said. She walked past them into the kitchen. She had changed out of her sweat shirts into a black turtleneck, making her skin look even darker than usual.

Jim lit Leena's cigarette and gave her back the lighter. She tossed it across the room, where it landed on the couch.

"It's true," Leena said. "All you want is the money."

"So what?" Beth asked.

"Well, maybe there's a lot of other people in this town who would like to be the winter carnival queen," Leena said. She blew smoke out of her nose and her mouth as she spoke. "I don't know why you have to keep coming back here and ruining everyone else's chances. You're the one who says you hate this town."

"The boys told me they'd be home," Beth said. She spread her makeup on the kitchen table and wiped the small compact mirror on a T-shirt hanging from the chair. "Where are they?"

"Your dad's up in the Copper Country doing snow removal," Leena said. She bent over the table, inspecting Beth's makeup. "He's been there since last Thursday."

"All right," Beth said. "But what about the boys? They knew I was coming home. Why aren't they around? Did they go out?"

"How would I know?" Leena asked. "They don't tell me anything." She picked up some of the makeup and carried it over to the window. As she looked at her reflection, she put on a thick layer of mascara, the cigarette glued to her bottom lip.

"All the attention you give them, couldn't you at least find out where they're going?" Beth asked.

"Your mother came and took all the furniture," Leena said. She stared at herself, turning her head slightly to one side. "I'm sure the boys helped her move everything out."

"It was her furniture," Beth said. "You knew she was going to take it one of these days."

"Not all of it was hers."

"She left what wasn't."

"Did you know she was going to come and take everything?" Leena asked. She put the mascara tube back on the table and reached for something else.

Beth slapped her wrist. "Leave it alone."

"Did your mother tell you she was coming over to take the stuff?" Leena waited until Beth was busy with the brush, combing out her hair, before picking up another stick of makeup.

"Maybe," Beth said.

"You let her know next time she steps foot in this house, I'm going to have her arrested," Leena said.

"It's her house," Beth said. "She bought and paid for it with her own money."

"It would have been nice if someone had let me know about her coming and stealing all the furniture," Leena said. She went back to her reflection in the window. "That way I would have been prepared for it. I almost died when I walked in and everything was gone."

Jim got tired of standing. He pulled out one of the chairs and sat down near Beth.

"What time is it?" She grabbed hold of his wrist and turned it to look at his watch.

"Almost eleven," he said.

Leena untied her shirttails and tucked them into her jeans. She unzipped her pants in the middle of the kitchen. "Maybe I'll go down to the bar with you two," she said.

Beth put her makeup back in the flowered case and rolled her eyes at Jim. Leena was quiet as if she expected Beth to tell her she couldn't go.

"You don't mind if I go to the contest with you, do you, Jim?" Leena put her coat on just as Beth was getting hers. "If Beth is in the contest, you'll just end up sitting alone anyway."

Beth pulled her hat on and walked out the front door, not waiting for either of them.

Jim got up and followed her out.

"Let her go," Leena said. "We'll be down at the bar soon enough. We'll see enough of her tonight."

He caught up with Beth on the street. "Wait a minute," he said. "What do you want me to do?"

"You might as well wait for her now," Beth said. "She's going to go no matter what."

"It's not my fault," Jim said. "What was I supposed to do?"

"You didn't have to talk to her," Beth said. "I told you to ignore her. That was the first thing I told you."

Beth went on ahead. Jim let her go. He let her get away with so much. But he wouldn't give up—not yet. Jim saw her slide down the path and reach for a branch to hold her balance. The trees were covered with ice and he was surprised when it didn't snap off in her tight grip.

It was close to one o'clock when they finally yelled, "On your mark, get set, go." The bartender had dropped the two cases of Mad Dog, carrying them up from the cold storage in the basement. Half the bottles broke, the cherry wine spilling everywhere. He tried to substitute blackberry Mad Dog, but some of the women protested, saying that two different flavors wouldn't be fair. One might be easier to swallow than the other. There was some talk about breaking into the liquor store down the street to replace the smashed bottles, but the judge argued that there had never been a rule about the wine having to be the same. The contest was the first woman to down the quart. Nothing had ever been said about flavor.

"There she is, front and center. Just like she always is." Leena nodded toward Beth, who stood in line with the other women on the dance floor, waiting for the contest to begin. The bar was hot with so many people. Beth fanned her face with a piece of paper.

Jim slid off his stool, giving it up to Leena. She had refused to sit down, waiting until Jim was sitting before pushing her hip against his leg, moving in on the stool.

"Does she think she'll win again?" Leena asked.

Jim drank his beer and shrugged. The coaster stuck to the bottom of his mug and he flipped it back on the bar.

"You can talk to me," Leena said. "Beth doesn't care if you talk to me."

Jim poured more beer in his mug and held the pitcher up for Leena. She pushed her glass over to him.

The bar smelled like cherry cough syrup. Jim kept his eyes on Beth. She had her hair tucked behind her ears, making her look young. Jim took another swallow of his beer and walked over to her.

"Good luck," he said. The noise in the bar was overpowering. She looked at him for a long moment and he wasn't sure if she was going to talk to him.

"I wouldn't stand so close if I were you," Beth said. "They go wild if they lose."

"What about you?" Jim asked. "Are you going to get wild?"

"I'm not going to lose," she said. She leaned forward to

speak to him while the woman next to her was yelling about drinking choke cherry wine. "But I'd like to get drunk."

"I'd like to see you get drunk too," he said.

"I'm sure you would."

"Do you want anything now?" he asked.

"I'd like this thing to get going so I can win and get out of here."

"How can you be so sure you'll win?" Jim asked. Her breath smelled like the stale cheese popcorn and she backed away as if she knew what he was thinking. He stepped closer to her.

"I didn't come up here to lose," she said.

The judge came by and collected the papers from the women. Jim looked at Beth in question.

"It's our head measurement," she said. "For the crown."

Jim laughed. He reached for her hand. She was sweating. He hadn't expected her to be nervous about the contest. He liked the feeling he had of protecting her, though he wasn't sure he was really doing anything. Beth wasn't the kind of person who seemed to need much protection.

"Why don't you tell Leena to get lost?" Beth said.

Jim kissed her and she pushed him away. He tried again and she let him kiss her for a couple of minutes.

"I mean it," Beth said, moving her face away from his. "It'll be big trouble if you give her a drop of attention. Pretty soon she'll be walking around with a swelled head and no one will be able to talk sense to her."

"I didn't know I had that kind of effect on women." Jim laughed.

"With someone like Leena, a dog could get her acting crazy."

The judge came back around and told the women to line up. The photographer from the *Baraga Bugle* was there to get a couple of pictures.

Jim went and sat down at the opposite end of the bar from Leena. He offered to buy the bartender a shot and the bartender gave him a free shot with a beer chaser. They toasted.

The bartender had white tape around his hand and held the beer mug with two fingers, his pinky wrapped immobile.

"You going to need stitches on that?" Jim asked.

"I don't think I got any glass in it," the guy said. He finished his shot and beer before Jim had taken a sip. Jim wondered if he was in training for the Jack Daniels contest.

The bartender leaned over to speak to Jim. "Do you know how much money I just made?" he asked.

Jim shook his head.

"Twenty bucks."

"For what?" Jim asked. For a split second he thought it might have something to do with Leena.

"The cases of Mad Dog," the bartender said.

The near-bald judge got up on one of the tables and called everyone's attention.

"What?" Jim asked. He turned his stool and saw Beth step up to the table.

"Yeah," the bartender said. He poured another half shot in both their glasses. "Some lady from Baraga paid me twenty bucks to drop the cases."

"I don't get it," Jim said. He swallowed his shot quickly.

"She gets sick on cherry," the bartender said. "But she really wants to win the contest."

The judge held the stopwatch over his head and called for quiet.

"Ladies, pick the bottles up," he yelled across the room.

Beth picked up the quart with one hand and gathered her hair off her face with the other. She held her hand on the back of her head as if giving herself support.

"Unscrew the caps," the judge screamed. "Get ready." He stared at the stopwatch. "On your mark, get set." He waited a second. "Go!"

Jim watched Beth. He saw her throw back her head and pour it all down at once. He knew she won when the judge jumped from the table and grabbed her arm. She threw the bottle to the ground. The judge held her arm over her head and said something, but the breaking of the glass muffled his words.

Leena came up behind Jim. She put her arms across his shoulder. "I don't know how, but she wins every year."

Jim inched away from her. "Do you want a beer?" he offered.

Leena nodded. "They shouldn't even let her enter," she said. "She should be disqualified the way she treats this town."

Jim lost track of Beth on the dance floor. Leena followed his stare across the room. "The Finns are going to go crazy. They wanted to win this year, but no one can pull that crown off that Indian's head. I guess it just goes to show you who the real drinkers are around here." Leena's makeup smudged under her eyes, her pale skin showing the blotted color.

"Maybe next year," Jim said.

"The Indians despise the Finns," Leena continued. "It has something to do with the land they say we took about two hundred years ago."

"I don't know," he said. He had heard the story from Beth. The Indians had been forced to move across Keweenaw Bay when the Finns came in to settle. Most of the Finns went to work in the copper mines, but some of them stayed and farmed the Indians' land. Jim didn't think Beth really cared about something that happened so long ago. He once asked her if that was why she had a grudge against Leena and she laughed. "That's why the Finns think we can't stand them, because they took our land. But we don't like them because they're stupid."

"Of course, that's not the only reason Beth hates me," Leena said. The bottles were still smashing on the floor and Jim had a hard time hearing what she was saying. "She thinks I'm turning her brothers away from her. But it doesn't have anything to do with me. They're wild."

The bartender came over and poured Jim another beer.

"Now that crazy woman wants her money back," he said.

"Just because she lost. I told her there was no guarantee on the deal, but she's stubborn."

"They're Indians," Leena said. "You know what they had in the living room when I first moved in?" She didn't wait for Jim's answer. "A spittoon. Right in the living room and when they watched TV they would spit in it. It made me so sick I had to throw it out. Now they spit in the sink, in the glassware, everywhere."

Jim drank his beer slowly, waiting for Beth to come over. He saw her and she held up her thumb. He raised his glass and she nodded.

"Are you in love with her?" Leena put her hand over his. He moved it to drink his beer.

"Why?" he asked.

"Because I can tell you right now, she's not in love with you."

"How can you tell that?" Jim asked. The woman next to him pushed up against him and he was caught off balance.

"Easy," Leena said. "If she was in love with you, she never would have brought you home. She never would have let you see where she came from."

Jim had already thought of that, so it didn't bother him to hear it from Leena. He wasn't sure he really believed it.

"And she sure wouldn't have let you see her chug a quart of Mad Dog," Leena continued. Jim moved away from the bar with his mug. The dance floor was covered with glass. The smell of the different flavors was suffocating. Beth was leaning on the railing talking to a group of guys, one of them probably the reigning Jack Daniels King.

The bathroom was empty. Jim stuck his mug on the sink and went into the stall. It was cool and quiet compared to the bar area. Only a couple of hours before, they had been complaining about the cold. Now his shirt was soaked with perspiration. He finished and went over to the sink. He closed his eyes and relaxed for a minute in the darkness. He was tired.

Leena walked in. He saw her blonde ponytail in the mirror.

"Is there a line for the girl's bathroom?" he asked.

She came over and put her arms around his neck.

"Don't," he said. "What are you doing here?"

He grabbed her wrist with his wet hands. She held tight, her own hands clasped together, pulling down his head.

"Don't worry," Leena said. She pushed her face against his, her skin brushing his cheek. "Beth's busy getting her photograph taken for the newspaper."

"Let go," he said. He pulled her hands apart and threw her away from him. Her head hit the paper towel dispenser as Beth walked in.

"Get out of here," Beth said. Jim bent over the sink and spit. The taste of whiskey was too thick in his throat.

Leena rubbed her head and glared at Beth.

"Get out of here," Beth yelled again. She moved toward Leena and Leena ran out.

"Do you know who she is?" Beth asked. She put her back to the door, blocking anyone's entrance.

"She walked in," Jim said. He washed his hands, letting the water pick up the spit on the side of the sink.

"She's my father's girlfriend," Beth said. "She sleeps with my father."

"She walked in and started making the moves on me," Jim said.

"Because you were paying her all that attention," Beth said. Jim had never seen her this frustrated and he wanted to believe that she was jealous. "You could have left her alone. You didn't have to talk to her."

"You're right," he said. "I should have ignored her."

"She's a Finn," Beth said. "Do you know what they do?"

Jim shook his head. "No. What do they do?"

"They store up for the winter like squirrels. They think squirrels have the right idea. In October they start eating as much as they can. They think that's smart. But do you know where that gets them?"

"No," Jim said. He went over and put his arms around her. "Tell me."

"It makes them fat," she said. "Really really big and fat." She was crying. Jim stroked her hair, pulling it from behind her ears. It fell in her face.

"Don't you see?" she asked. "If she tried something on you, then she tries things with my brothers."

"No," Jim said. "No, she doesn't." Jim held her close and she cried into his already damp shirt.

"She'll do anything to spite me," Beth said. "I told you to leave her alone."

"I'm sorry," Jim said. "I just didn't understand." He felt very close to her and hugged her into his chest. She let him hug her.

"I want to go back tonight," she said. She stood up straight and looked at her reflection in the mirror. Jim wiped a tear from one cheek and she turned her head so he could get the tears on the other cheek.

"I want to hitchhike back to Marquette," she said. "Will you go? I don't want to spend the night here."

"If that's what you want," Jim said. "You know that."

"I want to get out of here."

Leena was not at the bar when Jim walked back to get his jacket. Beth crossed the dance floor and went to the judge for her check. Jim spotted Leena near the jukebox in the front of the bar; when Beth was ready to leave, they went out the back door. They walked down the alley in silence.

"What about the ride on the float?" Jim asked. They turned the corner and the frozen Keweenaw Bay spread out in front of them, the white dead water illuminated in the dark night.

"I guess they'll have to find someone else to do it," Beth said. "It's not all that much fun anyway."

"Pretty cold up there?"

"It's freezing."

To the west, the gold painted statue of Bishop Baraga, the patron saint of L'Anse, watched over them from the low hills of the Porcupine Mountains. Their footsteps were muffled on the frozen gravel off to the side of the highway. The red taillights of the car flashed on fifty feet in front of them and Beth took off running. Jim ran, one more time, trying to catch up to her.

Miles from
Coconut Grove

Miles Lerner loved his job as letter man for the Coconut Grove Playhouse. From his stepladder perch, balanced against the marquee, he could see every inch of his beloved Grove. He thought it would be impossible to tire of watching the morning sun play rainbow games on the sailboats in Biscayne Bay, or walking near homes half-hidden by thick banyan leaves, or talking to Alfredo, the Bahamian boy who sold baggies of in-the-shell peanuts next to the magazine shop on Commodore Plaza. There was an easy rhythm to the Grove. Miles could hear it in the reggae-rock band that played at the Village Inn Bar until three in the morning. He felt safe walking home near dawn with the smell of ripe and rotting mangoes in the air. He liked the heat in the summer, the stillness of the winds off the ocean, the crowds at the beach on Key Biscayne, and the traffic coming off the Rickenbacker Causeway at night. He looked forward to December, when poinsettia plants grew on the walls of the private schools along Bayshore Drive.

Miles, like the rest of the Grovites, usually protested change. When the Cinga hotel chain moved in with its cranes and cement machines to build the Grand Bay Hotel, everyone was outraged. They felt they would lose everything they had if they allowed a high-rise hotel to be built. Miles wasn't sure how much it would change the Grove. While the others wrote letters to the editor of the *Coconut Grove News*, and organized demonstrations on Tigertail Drive, Miles kept quiet. He waited the eighteen months until the hotel was finished before saying anything.

On opening day he walked through the front lobby of the new Grand Bay Hotel to make his decision about the place. He admired the peach wallpaper, the full-length gold-spotted mirrors. The desk clerk smiled and Miles waved. He took the elevator to the top floor to have a look at the new nightclub, Regina's. There was talk around the Grove of the exclusiveness of the place, but Miles didn't believe anyone would open a bar which would keep out residents of the Grove. The main room was crowded with a cleaning crew that was vacuuming and rearranging low velvet chairs around triangular-shaped cocktail tables. The bar in the center had no liquor bottles on the glass shelves and Miles hoped they weren't going to use computerized drinks. He loved the different colored liquor bottles. The sun pouring from the overhead skylight cast uneven circles of light on the carpet. Miles moved in a circle, watching his shadow grow larger and then smaller again. A man in a mustard-colored jacket approached him.

"It's just beautiful," Miles said. He held out his hand and the man shook it.

"Welcome to Regina's," the man said. "Can I help you?"

"You've done a great job here," Miles said. "What a view you have!"

The man led him over to the window, where they could see the bay and the white masts of the sailboats lined along the docks. After a few minutes Miles thanked his host and took the elevator down to the pool level. When he stepped out into the open air, the intensity of the heat surprised and pleased him. He walked along the edge of the pool, following his reflection in the smooth, brittle water. The metal lounge chairs were painted the same pink as the silk bows tied to the base of the palm trees on the front lawn announcing the hotel's opening day. The bartender in the corner, wiping a rag along the empty rattan counter, flashed a white smile at him. Miles took off his shirt and dove into the pool. The water was ice-cold. He swam to the other side and stood in the shallow end, letting the sun dry his back.

"It's great," he called over to the bartender. "Wonderful."

The bartender pointed to a stack of folded towels on one of the lounge chairs. Miles pulled himself out of the pool and reached for a towel. He wiped his face in the lemon smell of the terrycloth and walked over to tell the bartender how much he approved of the whole thing.

Friday at noon Miles stopped off at the chicken shack. Tina, the owner of Wings and Things, started complaining about the hotel.

"It's not bad," Miles said. He got off his bicycle and set it against the side of the building. The night's thunderstorm and winds had pounded the unprotected building and chipped the paint. Spots of light green acrylic were scattered on the sand. "You should see it," he added. "They have a pool lined with ferns so you can't see the street."

"I like the street," Tina said. She sat inside the shack off to one side in the shade. Tina was always complaining about the heat. The stoves used all her electrical outlets and she couldn't put in a fan without shutting something down. When business got slow in the summer, Miles could ride by and see Tina asleep in the lawn chair, with only the hum of the stoves keeping the place alive. "I want people to see the streets. That's when they see the little businesses like mine."

"Go over and take a look at it," Miles said. He poured hot sauce on the dark side of the wing. "You'll love it. It's got to bring business to the Grove."

"I can see it from here," Tina said. "And I'm not happy with it."

Miles looked over his shoulder. The curve of the road, following the ocean, blocked the hotel from sight.

Tina watched him. "Well, I can feel it from here. I can't help hating it. The high-rises are going to ruin my business."

"More people should improve business," Miles said. He let the hot sauce bite into his lip for a moment before taking a sip of his soda.

"I've been thinking about Key West," Tina said. "Key West has the street traffic I need to make money."

"Everyone's a vegetarian in Key West," Miles told her. He didn't like the idea of Tina moving from Coconut Grove. She was one of the very first people he met when he arrived five years ago.

"That's not what I hear." Tina stood up and folded the lawn chair. "Do you have time to help me unload some heavy boxes? I've got an extra case of frozen fries for the bed race."

"Aren't you jumping the gun?" He hoisted himself up on the counter and swung his legs around inside the shack. "I always thought it was in March."

"Today's the eighth," Tina said. When he didn't respond, she added, "Of March."

The bed race was an annual event. Teams of four pushed a bed down a mile-and-a-quarter course through the Grove. Each team had to carry one person and keep her tucked inside the sheets. People came from as far away as Gainesville to compete.

"I've got to get A. J. to organize the team this year," Miles said. "We almost won last year."

Tina handed him a knife and he sliced through the heavy layers of tape sealing the box. "You guys didn't enter last year."

"The year before, then," Miles said.

"No. You were disqualified that year," Tina said. "Remember? One of your coasters fell off in front of the French restaurant."

"We got close one year," Miles protested.

"You guys never get it together to even come close to finishing. You know most of those teams train all year. I see Phil and his Budweiser Team running across the causeway every night."

"They cheat," Miles said. What he really liked about the bed race was the party afterward when the streets of the Grove were packed with people in shorts and T-shirts. The street vendors from Jamaica sold dollar bottles of Red Stripe beer at every corner. The Bahamian bands started playing after the awards ceremony and people danced until the sun stopped shimmering on the ocean and the blue water turned dark with the night.

Miles helped her stack the deep freezers with the frozen fries and Tina stuffed the rest in Styrofoam coolers. He dragged the coolers to the other side of the shack away from the stoves.

Tina wouldn't let him pay for his lunch and he rode off to the Coconut Grove Playhouse, forty-five minutes late for work.

Miles liked the musty odor that hit him when he walked into the theater. It smelled of years of salt blown in off the ocean and trapped in the wood. He went down to the storage area and stuck his head under the faucet. The cold water dripped down his neck and soaked his shirt. A paint-speckled tarp covered most of the room and he had to move it out of the way to get at the seven-foot ladder. During the season the plays changed every nine days. It was his job to keep the marquee current. Julian had a quirk about it and no matter how many times Miles complained, he insisted that the marquee be cleared completely—that Miles take down every letter. Most of the letters were reused, but Julian was stubborn. The letters had to be washed individually every time. If Miles protested, Julian lectured him about sea-grime and dust. Special attention had to be paid to vowels, especially the As and the Es: letters that were used in every show. Miles didn't see why Julian wouldn't let him bring the hose around to the front of the theater and wash the letters while they were still on the marquee. But since he was paid hourly, he took his time and did what Julian wanted.

Miles dragged the ladder outside and set it against the building. He unhooked the letters on one side and stacked them near the posters that announced the play opening that night—*The Glass Menagerie*. Miles usually went to see the plays at the first matinee. He liked the audiences in the afternoon—the tourists from Delray and Boynton Beach who applauded everything.

The sun dried his shirt quickly and the stiff cotton scratched his back. He pulled it over his head and tossed the shirt to the sidewalk. A. J.'s rusted white Le Mans drove by and then made a U-turn and circled back. He parked it in the theater parking lot and called out to Miles.

"You almost done?" A. J. was from New York. He had been

living in Coconut Grove two years longer than Miles, but he never let anyone forget where he was from.

"I just got started," Miles said. The last E on the side of the marquee was caught on the edge and he couldn't pry it loose. "Where you been, buddy?"

"Busy working," A. J. said.

Miles wiped the sweat from his hands down the sides of his jeans and continued to pull on the E. He was afraid of cracking the letter. The theater was always running out of vowels and then it would be up to Miles to shorten the play titles. "They hire you full time yet?"

A. J. worked at Miami International unloading fruits and vegetables off cargo planes in from the islands. The pay was good, but A. J. complained about the lack of hours and the flies.

"No," A. J. said. "And I don't think they're going to. I've been working on something new I want to show you."

"What is it?" Miles asked.

"Take a break. You've got to see it."

"Help me carry these," Miles said. "If you give me a hand, I can finish in no time."

Miles climbed down without the E, picked up two consonants, and stuck a third under his arm. A. J. carried a G and followed Miles around back to the parking lot. The letters were hot and Miles walked slowly, carrying them away from his bare skin. A few drops of rusty water trickled from the hose when he turned it on. The water pressure wasn't strong enough to rinse off any soap. Miles sprayed the top of the letters and stacked them against the stucco walls to dry. If Julian came by, he would think they were washed.

The floor of A. J.'s car was covered with fast food wrappers, empty oil cans, and socks. Miles put his feet on the dashboard and unrolled the window.

"I've got something going that's going to be worth a lot," A. J. said.

"So tell me," Miles said.

"I will. I will. Let's stop at the Commodore Plaza for something to drink," A. J. said as he pulled in front of the liquor store.

Miles ran in for a six-pack of beer. When he came out, Alfredo was sitting on the curb with two bags of peanuts. He held them up to Miles.

"Come on, Miles," Alfredo said. "Buy these from me."

Miles handed him two quarters.

"I want to buy some basketball laces," Alfredo said. "I need more than fifty cents."

"Keep the peanuts," Miles said. "Go sell them." He unscrewed the beer bottle and took a long swallow. The beer smelled like it was skunked. He got back in the car and A. J. pulled away from the curb.

Traffic was slow. Miles suggested walking down to the bay, but A. J. said he needed something from the trunk. They parked behind Wings and Things and Tina told them she'd meet them down by the docks after she made her day's deposit. The only bank in the Grove closed early. A. J. pulled a cordovan briefcase from the trunk.

"Are you going corporate on me?" Miles asked. He whistled as A. J. turned the briefcase around.

"Isn't it beautiful?" he asked.

"Sure," Miles agreed. "But what are you going to use it for?"

"I want to wait for Tina to show you," A. J. said.

Miles grabbed the six-pack and they walked down the path to the other side of the park close to the ocean. Miles stretched out on the grass and watched the kids near the overturned picnic tables toss a Frisbee back and forth. The breeze caught their voices and they seemed to play in silence. From the water, he could hear the clanging of the mast hooks hitting the booms. The sky overhead was the same clear blue as the ocean.

A. J. balanced the briefcase on his knees. "You heard anything from Suzanne?"

"I'm going to call her," Miles said. "Last time I talked to her she was thinking of coming down."

"For a visit?" A. J. asked. "Or to stay?"

Miles shrugged. Suzanne was his girlfriend, his used-to-be girlfriend. He still lived in the apartment they'd shared and they talked on the phone at least once a week. Suzanne was from Minneapolis, and after a while she had started to hate Coconut Grove. The heat made her cranky, and she never got used to the absence of seasons. After two years of trying to like the Grove, she gave up and moved home to Minneapolis. Miles kept thinking she'd come back in the winter and she did come, for an eight-day visit in October. They drove her rental car down to Key West for the Halloween Festival. Her skin burned—it blistered at the shoulders, and she couldn't go out in the sun. Miles told her he would go back up north with her. She said he wasn't serious. She wanted to know who would take care of the letters at the theater. He told her he hadn't meant he would leave during the season. He was talking about after April, when it would be summer up north.

"We can go back and forth," Miles reasoned. He had her plane ticket hidden between the mattress and box spring as she packed. He wanted to make her miss her plane. "We can spend the winters down here and the summers in Minneapolis."

"What about jobs?" Suzanne had asked.

"We can find them," he told her. "Julian will give me my job whenever I want it."

But she left, telling him she wanted to think about it. He found himself wondering at odd times why he didn't know what she was doing at a particular moment in the day. She laughed over the phone when he told her that. "You're always welcome to come up here and find out," she said.

"If she doesn't come down, I'll go visit her," Miles told A. J. But A. J. wasn't listening. Tina came up with a large Wings and

Things paper sack. "I thought you two might be hungry," she said. She sat down and set the bag between them. She slit through the grease stain with her fingernail and the paper tore away. She handed Miles a wing.

A. J. shook his head. He moved the briefcase from the wings and popped open the lock. Inside were fifteen serrated knives with flowered handles.

Tina smiled at him. "What are you doing with all those knives, A. J.?"

"It's my new job," A. J. said. "I'm going to be a salesman just like that guy in the play you took us to, Miles. I'm working for the Berkmar Knife Corporation. And I want you two to be my first customers."

"I don't need any knives," Miles said. He had seen *Death of a Salesman* nine times when it ran at the Playhouse.

Tina reached for a knife, but A. J. pulled the briefcase away.

"Wait," he said. "You have to listen to my speech." He took the paper from his pocket and stood up. The briefcase was balanced off his hip.

"Excuse me," he read from the paper. "Maybe you can help me. My name is A. J. and I'm with the Berkmar Corporation, which distributes a fine line of Cutto Cutlery. My job is to have some people in this area test this patterned cutting edge." A. J. put down the briefcase and pulled out a knife. He showed Miles and Tina the edge. "Would you be so kind as to give this knife a try overnight? Try it on a variety of things—fruits or vegetables or, if you're having meat for dinner, try it on that. I'll be back tomorrow to discuss your reaction."

"They keep the knives overnight?" Miles asked. He finished his beer and started another.

"Yeah," A. J. said. "That way there's no pressure for them to decide right then. They can try them out and we come back the next day and see if they want the set."

"What if they steal them?" Miles asked.

"We know where they live," A. J. said. "Tell me what you

think. I get a great commission. Don't you think that people
will buy?"

"But what if they don't give back the knives?" Miles protested. He threw his chicken bone over to the garbage can and
missed. He got up and tossed it in. "I mean, what if you go
back the next day and they refuse to return them?"

A. J. ignored Miles. "What about you, Tina?" he asked. He
took one of the knives from the maroon straps and handed it
to her. "Do you think you'd ever use a knife like this around
the shack?"

"I'm not sure, A. J.," she said. "I mostly just tear the chicken
apart with my hands. You know I wear plastic gloves and a
knife would slip out."

"Look at this," A. J. commanded. "The grip is really tight. It
would never slide through. Even with gloves you could still
grasp it."

"Where are you going to sell them, A. J.?" Miles asked. "In
the Grove?"

"I'm going to start here," A. J. said. He pulled the skin off a
piece of chicken and stuck it on the paper bag. Tina picked up
the skin and ate it. "But I'm worried about the high-rises. I
think people are going to start moving out. Just look at it. It
would make anyone move out."

They turned their heads to the Grand Bay Hotel. The sun
caught the glare off the top row of windows and Miles squinted
as he tried to imagine how such a beautiful building would
make people leave the Grove.

"That's what I was saying to Miles," Tina said. "There's no
room for businesses like us anymore. We have to clear out of
here."

"It's not such a bad place," Miles said. "Go take a look at it."

"One hotel's not bad, but wait until there's a whole row of
them blocking the bay. You won't be so happy about it then,"
A. J. said. He motioned down the road. "I can just see them all
stacked up next to each other."

"You ever think about Key West?" Tina asked. She wiped the

barbecue sauce off her fingers in the stiff crabgrass.

"Would you need a car down there?" A. J. asked. He straightened the knives in the case.

"Aren't there a lot of fishermen in Key West?" Miles said. "They're not going to use knives with flowered handles." He remembered when Suzanne was sick with sunburn in Key West, he had walked out along the south pier and watched the fishermen come in. He was impressed with their ropes and wooden cages and the smell of the sea. Later, when he was describing it to Suzanne, she asked about the kinds of fish they dragged in, and Miles had to tell her he hadn't noticed.

"Why don't you try a knife at the shack, Tina?" A. J. asked. "It might be the start of a great partnership."

"Do you really think you might be interested in Key West?" Tina motioned to the briefcase and A. J. turned it around for her inspection.

"No one's going to buy knives in Key West," Miles said. "They're all tourists."

"They buy everything in Key West," A. J. said.

"Let me try the knife," Tina said. "Maybe I'll strike it rich at the bed race this year and actually have enough money to move the shack."

Miles shut his eyes against the glare and in the grayness heard the sound of a plane passing overhead.

A. J. must have heard it too, because he closed his briefcase and stood up. "I have to get out of here. I'm working second shift at the airport tonight."

They took a shortcut across the park through the Frisbee game. Tina carried the knife against her leg and Miles watched the blade, afraid it would cut into her skin.

"What about Sunday?" Miles asked. "Will you think about racing, A. J.?"

"If I sell some knives tomorrow," A. J. said. "I guess I could always sell them at the bed race. People might go crazy over the knives there."

Miles didn't see how A. J. could carry around the cordovan

briefcase at the bed race. It was enough of a problem to find a place to put the empty bottles of Red Stripe when the music started. Last year Miles had lost his bicycle in all the confusion. He was sure he had tied it to the tree in front of Señor Frogs, but when he finally went to get it, the bike wasn't there.

Back at the theater, the stage crew had finished setting up for the first scene. Miles vacuumed the aisle, picking up papers and soda cans. Julian came in annoyed because he couldn't find a substitute for the ticket-taker who had quit after the last show. Miles volunteered, knowing he could leave by nine or stay and watch the show for free. Julian found him an extra-large tuxedo shirt and a pair of black pants. Miles changed in the bathroom and hid his clothes in the storage closet. Then he went downstairs to the pay phone and dialed Suzanne's number in Minneapolis collect. He was surprised when she answered on the first ring. She hesitated with the operator about accepting the charges.

"You busy?" Miles asked.

"No," she said. "Just surprised you called collect."

"I'm at work," he said. He held the phone away from his ear as if he could show her the theater, have her smell the heavy odor of hair spray from the makeup rooms.

"You can put money in those machines," she said. "Quarters and dimes and things like that."

He ignored her sarcasm. "I heard it's pretty cold up there," he said. "The map in *USA Today* had everything above Chicago colored white."

"It's not that bad," she said.

"It's 85 and sunny down here," he said.

"Isn't it always?"

"Maybe," Miles said. He ran his fingers up and down the starched white ruffles of the tuxedo shirt.

"What are you doing?" Suzanne asked. "What's new in the Grove?"

"I'm trying to decide which beach to go to tomorrow," he said. He pulled the phone cord around to give it enough slack so he could sit on the table. "I can't decide between Sonesta Beach, where I know we can rent windsurfs free, or South Beach. Did I tell you A. J.'s brother's working at the sailboat rental out there?"

"Yes," Suzanne said.

"But I also like South Beach. They have a band that plays out there now. Right on the sand."

"You should be able to make that decision in an instant," she said.

"It doesn't sound easy to me," Miles said.

"No?" she asked. "You've been making it every week for the last five years."

Miles didn't say anything. It would have been better to call her after work, when he wasn't uncomfortable in the warm building, when the tuxedo pants weren't pressing into his stomach. He could have called her from the pay phone near the Village Inn, where she'd hear the music and he could have described the people passing by.

"I'm sorry, Miles," she said. "I don't want to be mean. It's just that you're always telling me about the same thing. Every time you call, you tell me A. J.'s brother is working at the Sonesta."

"He just got the job at Christmas," Miles said. He undid the first button of his shirt and scratched his neck.

"Right," she said. "And that's when you started telling me about it."

"You talk then," Miles said. "Tell me what you've been do-ing. Tell me what's going on at work."

"Work is good," Suzanne said. "I'm thinking about going with a group from the office to the Yucatán in April."

"I thought you were coming down here," Miles said.

"No," Suzanne said. "You said you were coming up here this spring."

"Maybe," Miles said. "Maybe I should." He tried to remember if he had told her about the Grand Bay Hotel, about *The Glass Menagerie*, about A. J.'s new job. But instead he filled the silence with a promise to call her again later that night.

"Not too late," she warned.

Miles stayed for the show and left the theater after midnight. The streets were jammed with locals. He admired the women in the bright-colored high heels. They didn't wear nylons and their legs glistened in the bluish hue of the streetlights. Miles rode home the long way, around Bayshore Drive. A spray caught in the night wind blew in from the ocean. He got off his bike and turned his face to the water. The wind wet his skin and he licked the salt off his lips. The bus stop across from the Grand Bay Hotel wasn't lit and the voice caught him by surprise.

"Hey," someone called to him. "Hey there. When does the bus run?"

He walked his bike closer to the figure hidden in the shadows. A young girl was sitting on the bus bench. She wore a white uniform and clean, almost fluorescent white shoes. "What time is the next bus?" the girl asked.

"There isn't one," Miles said. "It's too late."

"Are you sure?" She had her purse on her lap and both arms wrapped around it.

"The last one runs at midnight," Miles said.

"How am I going to get home?" The girl brushed her hair off her forehead. They were both getting wet in the ocean spray.

Miles set his bike against the banyan tree where the thick roots helped support it. "Aren't you too young to be working so late?"

"I work at the Grand Bay," the girl said. "We had a wedding and the reception was really long."

"Take a cab," Miles said. "Why don't you take a cab home?"

"I only have bus fare," she said.

Miles put his hand in his front jean pocket and felt the crumpled twenty-dollar bill he'd put there that morning. "Do you live far?" he asked.

"Kendall," the girl said. "I live in Kendall."

Miles handed her the money. "Take a cab home," he said.

"No." She held the bill out to give back to him.

"It's okay," he insisted. "Really.

The lights from the hotel were too high to illuminate the street, but the girl moved out of the shadow and Miles saw her face. Her small forehead was scrunched with worry.

"Where do I get a cab?" she asked. She folded the bill and stuck it in her uniform pocket.

"Call for one," Miles said. "The number's easy. 777-7777."

"Where?"

"Go in the hotel," he said. "I'm sure they have phones there. Come on. I'll go in with you."

They walked across the street, up the gold-lined steps to the lobby. A few people dressed for the evening sat with drinks in the overstuffed chairs. Miles went up to the desk clerk and asked him where the pay phones were. The desk clerk smiled and looked at the girl.

"You're here awfully late," he said.

"I missed my bus," she said. "I have to take a cab home."

"Let me call one for you," he said. He turned to Miles. "After all, we have to take care of our people."

Miles smiled. He reached for a pack of matches which had a drawing of the hotel on one side and the telephone number in large pink letters on the opposite side. The girl walked over to the glass outer doors and a man in a white tuxedo jacket approached her. Miles thanked the desk clerk and walked across the shiny floors.

"This is my manager." She introduced Miles.

"I'm Miles," he said. "Miles from Coconut Grove." They shook hands.

"Let me pay for your cab ride," the manager said. "I didn't

realize you had to take a bus home. I would have let you go early. I feel bad."

"That's okay," Miles said. "I got it."

"No, no," the manager said. "I insist." He reached in his pocket and pulled out his wallet. "How much do you think it will cost?"

"It's all right," Miles said. "She's safe."

The manager shook his hand again and said good night to the girl. He held the door open and Miles walked the girl out to the circular drive. He told her about the windsurfing off Key Biscayne and about the parrots that lived in flocks in the trees guarding the entrance to the Grove. He told her about Tina's chicken stand and about Ransford, who swept the streets at four o'clock in the morning with his long-handled broom.

When the cab pulled up, Miles held her arm. "Why don't you stay for a while? I can show you around. We can go to the Village Inn. You'll love the music."

The girl laughed. "I can't go anywhere like this." She looked down at her uniform. "People would think I was crazy if I went dressed like this."

"Not here," Miles said. "No one cares about that here."

"Another time," the girl said. "I'll be in the Grove almost every day this week."

"How about Sunday?" Miles said. "We can go to the bed race. We'll drink Red Stripes."

"Red Stripes?" The girl got in the cab and unrolled the window. "What's that?"

"You'll see," Miles promised. He ran after the cab. "You're just going to love the Grove."

The driver honked the horn, but Miles kept up with the cab. "I can't wait to show it to you. I'll be here," he called. The cab turned the corner at the next block and Miles chased after it for a minute before running back to the hotel.

He got on his bike and rode to the theater. The crew was still working and the radio echoed across the empty stage. He let himself into the storage room and dragged the stepladder out to the marquee. Shafts of light illuminated the sign—*The Glass Menagerie*. He studied it carefully and then balanced the ladder against the side of the building. He climbed up and looked out across the bay where he could see the outline of the sailboats anchored offshore. He turned back to the marquee and began pulling down some of the letters. The headlights of the passing cars gave him enough light so that he could see what he was doing. The letters were heavy and he was careful not to lose his balance as he stacked them together on the sidewalk. He stared at the marquee.

L S ME   I

He climbed back up the ladder and took his time rearranging the letters. He would fix it before Julian came to work in the morning. But for now it would stay so everyone could see it. He stepped down to inspect his work.

MILES

He stood on the curb facing the ocean and stared out across the still water. "It's not just tonight," he said aloud. He cupped his hands over his mouth, like a megaphone. "It's forever," he shouted. "Miles in the Grove. In the Grove forever Miles."

He would never leave.

The Seeney Stretch

He says the gray skies confused him. Surrounded by the trees losing their fall colors, the leaves almost all gone, my husband shot Colin.

"I was a hundred feet away," Patrick says. He stands in front of the fireplace, one foot on the brick hearth and his long arm stretched along the mantel. "Why didn't he say something? How come he didn't see me?"

Two policemen sit side by side on the couch. Their pressed blue pants have identical creases running down their legs. They hold matching coffee cups and only the one's blond mustache reminds me that I am not looking at a mirrored image. He asks Patrick to tell them again what happened just before he fired the gun. There is nothing cold about their questioning. They are hunters too. Duck, not deer, and they understand the silence of the woods, the sharp rustle of a sudden noise.

"I should have seen him," Patrick says. "His face at least. Why didn't I see his face?" Patrick puts his head in the crook of his arm and talks to the floor. He is still wearing his long underwear shirt, and the collar is dirty from sweat. He has been answering questions for almost twenty-four hours. First up in Marquette County and now down here, but I don't see any sign that he is tiring. His energy scares me because no matter how many times he tells it, I don't believe the story of the gray skies.

The policeman without the mustache leans forward and takes a white powdered doughnut from the tray. "It doesn't make any sense," he says. "Third day of deer hunting and the kid's wearing his vest in his jean pocket. What was he doing? Asking for it?" He bites into the doughnut and the crumbs fall onto his chest.

Patrick took Colin deer hunting up north near the Seeney Stretch. The land is dense with birch and poplar trees and the hunters wear orange vests so they can be spotted miles away.

The policeman turns to me, the crumbs balanced on his shirt. "We're not sure if Colin got lost or what. He could have ended up back at camp by mistake," he says.

I nod. My legs are crossed and I push against the floor with my heel, letting all the weight go back in the chair. The thick carpet muffles the noise.

"Was Colin having any problems?" the other policeman asks. "You know, like the runs, diarrhea? Did he get drunk the night before?"

"We had some beers the night before," Patrick says. "But not that many. Everyone just kind of fell asleep after an hour or two."

"Is there any reason you can think of why he didn't stay with John or that group?" The policeman coughs and sits forward.

"I don't know," Patrick says. He moves away from the fireplace and paces in front of the bay window. "He seemed okay. Maybe bored with the whole idea of hunting. I thought he'd like it, but it was really cold. It rained the whole time we were up there."

"The other group can't remember when Colin disappeared," the policeman says. "All of a sudden they realized he wasn't with them."

Without asking if anyone wants more, I go into the kitchen to start another pot of coffee. I pull the filter tray out slowly, listening to their conversation. I want the policemen to feel comfortable. No awkward empty cups. Outside, the rain catches in the wind and beats rhythmically on the storm windows. The coffee drips into the pot. A dirty brown color, it becomes rich only after the pot fills past halfway. I take the washcloth hanging on the faucet and wipe up the spilled granules on the countertop.

I thought the affair would end once I started teaching again in September, but the second week of school he was sitting on the back steps with a black and orange cat in his arms. He sat quietly, petting the cat's head, making a small clicking noise with his tongue.

"I have to get rid of her," he said without looking up at me.

"She's been hanging around our house for a month and my mom wants her gone before it gets too cold. I thought you might want her."

"Patrick's allergic to animal hair," I said. "We can't have any pets in the house." I was always mentioning Patrick to Colin, but he ignored or seemed to ignore the fact that I was married. "Can you take her to the humane society?"

"They won't take stray cats," he said. "Not without money."

"What are you going to do with her?" I asked.

The cat jumped out of his lap and began to explore a small pile of leaves under the steps. Colin unzipped his leather jacket. It was too warm a day to be wearing such a heavy coat, but I stopped myself from saying anything. Colin had told me he bought the coat because he thought it made his shoulders look bigger.

The cat knocked her head on the steel bar under the lawn chair and it collapsed. The sudden noise frightened her and she ran under the table. Colin went over and picked her up.

"You're getting heavy," he said. "I wonder if you're pregnant." He held her up in the air and then tucked her inside his jacket, turning her around so her head stuck out at his chest.

"You're going to take her on your motorcycle?" I asked. I moved closer to him, touched by his display of tenderness. "I don't think that's a good idea." I could hear the teacher in my voice.

"Why not?" he asked. He balled his fist and swatted it in front of the cat's face. She tried to grab at him, knocking her paw in the air—she hit at nothing. "Won't you, girl? You'll be okay. I'll take her down the highway a mile or so. There's a new subdivision where I can drop her off."

"She's got claws," I said. "You take her like that all trapped inside and she'll attack your chest."

"Do you think she'll be scared?" The urgency in his voice surprised me.

"Yes," I said. "Let me take you in the car."

It was the first time we had ever gone anywhere together. I thought it would be all right because of the cat. I could always tell Patrick I was just helping Colin get rid of the cat.

Colin kept her on his lap until we got to the highway and then let her into the back seat. He bent forward and turned on the radio. He flipped back and forth, along the stations, listening to a song for a minute before switching.

We drove to the construction site where the new roads were caked with wet mud. The afternoon had started to cool down and I rolled up my window.

"This is good," Colin said. We had pulled into a circular court, where the basements of the new homes had been sunk and sections of plywood were strewn on the cleared land. "We can drop her off here." He turned around to the back seat and started making the clicking sound with his tongue again.

"No one's living around here," I said. "They haven't moved in yet."

"She'll be okay. She's not afraid of squirrels or rabbits or anything."

"But there's nothing to eat here," I said. "She'll starve to death."

"Let me drive," he said. "I'll show you a good place. It's further down the road, toward the parkway, where they haven't started building."

"You don't want me to drive?"

He shook his head. I stopped the car and moved over to the passenger side. Colin didn't get out of the car. He brought his hand up to my neck and made a circular pattern on my cheek with his finger. I could smell the fresh leather of his jacket. The top button of my blouse was loose and he played with the thread until it fell off into his hand. He stuck the button in his mouth and showed it to me between his teeth.

"You can take your shirt off here," he said. "No one will ever see us out this far."

Usually when we made love I kept something on. It had

nothing to do with getting caught, although I had implied this to Colin. I didn't want him to see me naked. I already knew his legs were shorter than mine, that his hipbones fit inside mine.

I put my finger up to his lips and he drew his breath in, sucking my finger with the button. His teeth were sharp and it hurt. I pulled my finger out and let him undo the rest of the buttons on my shirt. The cat crawled along the top of the seat near our heads. Colin picked her up and tossed her in the back seat. He took off his jacket and folded it on the dashboard. The car stayed warm in the afternoon sun. He pushed at my shoulders until we both slid down the seat, our legs caught under the steering wheel. He closed his eyes, the skin around them creasing with concentration. When the car horn blew, we both tried to sit up right away. He was on top of me and I only caught a glimpse of the car—a funny orange color—before his weight crushed me back down into the seat. I grabbed my shirt off the car floor and put it between us. My heart was racing.

"I know that car," Colin said. He kept his head up, staring out the window. "But I can't tell who's driving."

"Is it Patrick?" I asked.

"No," he said. "Who drives that car?"

"Are you sure it's not Patrick?" I pushed him off me and pulled my shirt on. I started doing the buttons, my fingers too nervous to pull them through.

"Positive," Colin said. He sat all the way up, turning around to look out the back window. I heard the car pull away.

"Are they gone?"

"I think it was this kid from school," he said. "I'm pretty sure that's his dad's car."

"Did he see you?"

"Yeah," Colin said. He reached for his jacket and pulled it on without his shirt. The cat jumped in the front seat and began pulling at the plastic strings wrapped around the steering wheel.

"Colin," I said. "You don't tell people about us, do you?"

He shrugged.

"Do you, Colin?"

"No one that would care," he said. He looked down at himself. The dark leather against his pale skin. "This is how Jack Nicholson wears his jacket. I wouldn't mind looking like him."

I sat up and finished buttoning my shirt. I was ashamed, imagining how I would ever explain that he was nineteen. Colin sat beside me, talking about wanting to act like Jack Nicholson. I made a promise that I would stop it. I would just stop it. I told him to put his shirt on and I dropped him and the cat off around the block from his house. But the affair was still going on when Patrick surprised me and told me he had invited Colin to go deer hunting.

The coffee makes a finishing noise and I carry it straight into the living room. The steam travels quickly and hits my chin. I put my hand on the top of the pot, holding it there, until it burns.

"Just another mystery," the policeman says. "Seems like with hunting accidents, there's always something no one can explain."

I walk around and fill their cups. Three doughnuts are left on the tray and I pass it around too, but no one takes one. Patrick is sitting in the rocker. With his head back on the green pillow, he stares across the room at the policeman.

"Last year we had a real hunting mystery around here," the policeman continues.

"That's right," his partner agrees. "Right in this area. There was a father and son team who headed out first Thursday of the season. They were supposed to be up near Gaylord by midnight. They packed the car and drove down the driveway and that's the last anyone saw of them."

He pauses and both policemen shake their heads.

"What happened?" I ask.

"Disappeared," the policeman says.

"Did they find them in the woods?" I sit down on the carpet beside Patrick. He rubs his stocking feet together. I put my hand over the arch of his foot to make him stop moving. His nervous energy reminds me of a kid.

"Never found either of them. Ever," the policeman says. "No explanation. Nothing. Not even a real clue."

His partner finishes the story. "The case has been open for a year. A year and four days and we don't know any more now than we did when we first started investigating."

"But was it a hunting accident?" Patrick asks. He gets up from the rocker and moves back to his place in front of the fireplace. He knocks the painting crooked when he leans closer to the mantel. "How do you know it had anything to do with deer hunting?"

"Maybe not," the policeman says. "But it sure started out that way." He looks over at his partner and nods. The two of them get up, just when I thought they would stay all afternoon.

Patrick walks them to the door.

"Accidents happen every year," the tall one says to Patrick. "You'll go crazy if you start blaming yourself. It just happened. It's no one's fault."

He calls Patrick "buddy" and I hear Patrick laugh. I think they are playing games with each other, each telling the other that everything will be all right.

I crawl across the room and rub the doughnut powdered sugar into the carpet. The front door is open and the sound of the rain on the cement disguises the rest of their conversation. I breathe in slowly, refusing to let the panic take over. I am afraid Patrick wants to tell me that he shot Colin on purpose and I don't want to hear it, even if it's true. The door slams; with nothing to do with my hands, I kneel and reach for a doughnut. Patrick comes back into the room. When he touches the end table for his coffee cup, I can hear the static shock.

"Do you think you could sleep?" I suggest to him in the

silence of the room. "You look exhausted." It's not true but I want to be alone. It makes me nervous to be around him.

"I'm not tired," he says. He finishes the coffee and then plays with the cup, balancing it on the back of his hand.

"You must be," I tell him. "There are some sleeping pills in the bathroom. Your mother left them last time she was here. I'm sure it would be safe to take those."

"No," he says. "I don't want to be out of it."

"But you should try to sleep," I say. "It'll be quiet. I can unplug the bedroom phone."

I collect the coffee cups and pile them on the doughnut tray. I carry them into the kitchen and a second later Patrick follows. He won't look at me, but talks to the wall, right above my head. I sense his fear of being alone, but also the unease he feels at being with me.

"I want to talk to John," he says. "I want to know what the police are telling him."

"Why?" I ask. "Why should it be any different than what they're telling you?"

"Because I'm the one who fired the shot," Patrick says. He stretches his arms over his head and rests them on top of the door frame.

"Do you think there's something they're not telling you?" I ask.

"Not you too, Jessie," he begs. "I've got everyone asking me questions. I don't need you too."

"I'm sorry," I say. "I didn't mean anything by it." I dump the rest of the coffee into the sink and put the cups in the dishwasher. It is nearly full. I get out the soap from under the sink. It's a new box and I can't open the silver triangle on the side of the package. I take a dirty knife from the basket and try to pry it open. Patrick holds out his hand for the box and I give it to him.

"I just don't understand." I stop myself from saying anything more.

"What?" Patrick asks slowly. "What don't you understand?"

"Why did you have to take him hunting at all?" I say. "I don't understand why you had to bring him up there in the first place."

"Jessie," he yells. "Jessie. Colin was a kid. I took him hunting because I thought it would be good for him."

The word "kid" stings in my ear. Patrick's face is white and I am afraid to look at him because I can hear him crying now. I stare at a stain on the floor in front of his feet.

"I thought he'd like to go hunting," Patrick yells. He throws the unopened box of detergent on the counter and walks to the back of the house. The bedroom door slams. A minute later I hear the radio. He never falls asleep when he listens to music.

I go out to the garage without my coat. It smells of bleach from when I tried to get rid of the oil spots in the middle of the floor. Protected from the rain and cold, I wander around looking for a T-shirt of Colin's. He left it in the house one afternoon, walking home in his cutoffs. When I found it two days later stuffed under the couch, I threw it in the garage. As I walk around, I start throwing things away in the open trash can: a month-old newspaper, a paintbrush without a handle. His T-shirt is hidden behind the lawn rake, dirty with fall leaves. I pick it up and whisper his name. It's soft against my cheek. I kiss the cotton, trying to bring him close to me once more.

It was the first week in June. The heat had come without warning, following two months of cold spring.

"I need a rag or something," he said. He had knocked on the back screen door and then called out when I didn't hear him. "I cut my foot."

"How bad is it?" I asked. The back door was usually kept closed and it took me a few seconds to find the latch. The lock was tight. The silver knob pressed into the soft skin under my thumbnail when I released it. "Is it bleeding?"

"I think so," he said. He ran his tongue back and forth over his front teeth. The heat was dry.

I didn't know his name, but I told him to come into the kitchen where I could look at his foot. He sat down on the chair in the corner instead of at the table. It's a kid's stool left over from the woman who sold us the house. I use it to reach the cupboards above the stove.

"Take it off," I said. "Let me look at it. Maybe whatever it is is still in your foot."

I turned on the faucet and let the water run warm before wetting the washcloth. Blades of grass clung to his bare ankles and he brushed them off onto the linoleum. I held the damp cloth against his foot for a minute and then looked at the cut.

"Do you think it needs stitches?" he asked.

I knelt in front of him and pushed the skin around the cut, soaking the cloth with blood.

"Can you feel anything in there?" I asked. "Does it hurt?"

"Not really," he said.

The skin pulled away from his foot. "Is it glass?" I asked.

"I don't know," he said. "It shot into my foot. At first I thought it was a stick, but then I felt the blood."

He pulled his T-shirt over his head, grabbing it up from the back. He brought it up to his face and dried the sweat on his forehead and then ran the T-shirt down his stomach, following the dirty lines of sweat on his skin.

"It's my brother who usually does your lawn," he said. "He's the one that should be here, but he's still at hockey camp."

I remember looking at his chest. It was pink from the heat. There was one drip of sweat around his nipple and I moved my hand to wipe it off. He grabbed my wrist when I touched his skin.

"What's your name?" I asked.

"Colin," he said.

He was still holding my wrist when he took his T-shirt and brushed it back and forth across his chest. He shivered and his nipples hardened.

"Are you older?" I asked. I couldn't remember what his brother looked like.

"My brother's only fifteen."

"That's right," I said.

"I just turned nineteen," he said. "I'm legal now if you ever want to go out for a beer."

"Really?" I said. "Go out for a beer?"

"Sure." He shrugged and I knew he was embarrassed.

I had to do it. I pulled my wrist from his grasp and touched his skin above his breastbone. He pulled away in surprise. He was so young, so surprised at my touch that when I saw him blush, his cheeks flamed with uncertainty, I kept my hand on his chest. I let my fingers move slowly back and forth over his nipple. The fine hair dampened with sweat. If he hadn't closed his eyes I would have stopped, but he relaxed in the stool and I let my hand move up to his neck and he dropped the T-shirt and when he touched me, I pulled his head down to mine.

Patrick came home two hours later. I was out on the deck, just standing there. The wood slats were warm beneath my feet. He asked me what I was doing and I told him I was looking for a sparkler or a nail. I told him Colin cut his foot mowing the lawn.

"His name is David," Patrick told me.

"No," I corrected him. "That's his brother." The sun was hot and I put my hand on the patio table for support.

The affair had been going on for more than a year when Patrick walked into the living room one night with one of the bathroom towels. My hair was still wet from the shower I had taken after Colin left.

"This smells like sex," he told me.

"It's our towel," I told him. "Why should that surprise you?"

"Smell it." He put the towel to my face and I could smell Colin in the damp terrycloth.

"So what?" I pushed it away and went back to reading the magazine.

"Are you sleeping with someone?" he asked. His face was drawn, and I found it painful to look at him.

"Is it David?" he asked. He brought the towel up to his face again as if he could discover who it was.

"David?" I had been thinking of Colin and when he said David I thought of Colin's brother. It took me a minute to realize he was talking about one of our neighbors, a good friend of Patrick's who had recently been laid off from his job. He was home during the day and his wife worked. "David Enderby?" I said. "Of course not."

He didn't mention it again, but one time I found him looking through the pockets of my raincoat and, when I asked him what he was doing, he shook his head. "Protecting myself," he said. "Just protecting myself."

"Protecting yourself from what?" I asked.

"Against surprise," he said.

I knew what he was talking about, but I dropped the subject. I'm not sure how Patrick found out about Colin. But I was positive he knew. It was something in the way Patrick continually brought up Colin's name. It was the way he treated Colin like a child—the way he kept reminding me that Colin was young, someone who was harmless, someone who had no effect on our lives, but someone who was just there, like a toy.

The house is getting dark, but I refuse to put on any lights. I want to stall the night. In the living room, I flip the cushions on the couch over and the crumbs fly to the floor. I sit down and face the window. Outside, the street lights are not lit; the day hangs on. There is a film of dust which always comes with the winter. I wipe it off and brush it down the side of my jeans. My hands are dry. I suck on my finger until the nail softens. I bring my teeth down on the nail and feel it give. It hurts when I rip it off. I spit it on the rug. My hand looks uneven as I hold it in front of my face. The skin is raw and I bite the rest of my nails, tearing them off until all my fingers hurt.

The shadows in the room shift, and Patrick is standing in the doorway watching me.

"Couldn't you sleep?" I ask.

"No," Patrick says. He comes over to the couch. I can't see his face until he kneels in front of me. "What am I going to do, Jessie? What should I do?"

Colin's T-shirt is in my lap and I tuck it under my leg. "Don't," I say. "Don't think about it."

He puts his head in my lap and I can feel the dampness of his tears through my jeans. He rubs his face in my legs. I reach up to turn on the lamp and he lifts his head. The dark circles under his eyes show for the first time.

"It's all right," I tell him. "It's going to be okay." I take his hand and we stand up together. He follows me down the back hallway to the bedroom. The blanket is pushed to the end of the bed. I sit and turn the radio down. Patrick takes his clothes off before lying beside me. I hear the change from his pocket as it falls on the wood floor. Patrick is very strong and his weight crushes my chest, but I do not move. His face rests at my neck and I still feel his tears. My muscles tense. I hold him tight and come right away. I keep my hands on the back of his neck and we stay together until he shivers and moves off me.

Patrick turns to the wall. His breathing quiets after a moment. In the silence, I try to imagine the woods, the spidery trees against the sky, the dull color in the air from seventeen days of rain. It reminds me of when Patrick and I went camping in the Upper Peninsula and first discovered the land around the Seeney Stretch. The man at the Mackinac tollbooth warned us about the fires.

"They're right at the Seeney Stretch," the man said. "Always has been a problem spot."

We told him we didn't know where it was.

"Two hours north of here," he said. "Just when you think you can't stay awake any longer you'll hit the Seeney Stretch. It's a thirty-eight-mile straightaway. Drives the truckers crazy.

They're always driving off the road. Think they see something. A light or something shining on the road."

The day was bright with sunshine. Patrick and I thanked the man for the warning. As we got closer to the park entrance, the sky clouded over. Patrick predicted rain. We lost sight of the horizon, driving deeper into something we couldn't see. A state trooper on the side of the road flagged us down and told us about the fires. They had been burning underground for months, he said. The dry summer was bringing them above ground and the grass and trees were burning faster than the fire fighters could control them. The police were afraid for the deer, who were too scared to run from the flames. The heavy smoke made the land look like the end of the world. We drove down the straightaway, counting off the miles on the odometer. Patrick had to drive under the speed limit to keep the car on the road. The entrance to the park was clouded over from smoke, like a fog that wouldn't lift. We stopped for only a minute, deciding to drive north into an area Patrick knew from hunting. I wanted to get away from that stretch of land as quickly as we could. By Munising, the sky had cleared and we camped at Picture Rocks on Lake Superior, the clear blue water letting us forget what was behind.

Lunch at Archibald's

The first thing Colleen thought when she saw her ex-husband's new wife at Archibald's was that Leah was following her. It was too much of a coincidence for Leah to be in the same out-of-the-way restaurant at the same time as Colleen. The move was typically Leah—something only she would try and pull off. But Leah, whose hair was bleached white-blonde in the summer months, didn't even glance at Colleen as she crisscrossed through the dining room on her way to the Ladies' Room. Colleen hesitated. She spread her accordion-shaped napkin on the table and pressed the creases with her palm before getting up to confront Leah.

"Colleen. Where are you going?" Her sister Tricia stopped her at the host stand. "I've been waiting up here for ten minutes. Did you already get a table?"

"Leah's in the bathroom," Colleen whispered. She pointed to the alcove where the figures on the two doors were painted the same maroon as the carpeting.

"Is that why we're eating lunch here?" Tricia moved to the other side of Colleen, blocking the door to the bathroom.

"Didn't you see her? She just walked by. Two seconds before me."

"Why don't we get out of here?" Tricia asked. "We can eat at the deli across the street."

"How could you miss all that bleached blonde hair going by?"

"Let's go," Tricia said. "The deli is never crowded. We'll get served right away."

"I want to say something to Leah." Colleen tucked in the front of her blouse and pulled her locket around straight so the clasp was at the back of her neck where it belonged.

"Leave her alone," Tricia said. She took hold of Colleen's elbow and pulled her away from the line of people waiting to be seated. "Don't make a fool of yourself."

"Go sit down," Colleen said. "It's the last table on the window side."

"Is George with her?" Tricia tightened her grip on Colleen's elbow, catching her nail on the knit of her sweater. "Don't tell me he's here too."

"No. She's with a woman." Colleen looked over Tricia's shoulder to the bathroom.

"I mean it, Colleen. No scenes."

Colleen nodded. She knew her sister would leave if there was a fight. Tricia had been with her when she and George met at First Federal Bank to sign the papers when they sold the house. Colleen had been having a bad day and she wasn't sure why she started yelling at George in front of the loan officer. Tricia had been mortified and fled to the parking garage to wait out the fight. Colleen never told her about the incident at the water fountain. George had run to the elevators without saying a word to her. The loan officer had walked her out to the car.

Colleen moved out of Tricia's hold and walked back to the table. The busboy in a red tuxedo jacket, the top two buttons missing, stood over the table refolding the linen napkin. Colleen took it from him and sat down.

Leah William had been George's mistress for almost two years. And despite everything Colleen had done to stop it, Leah became his second wife on Valentine's Day. Colleen was positive she would still be married to George if the affair had been kept a secret. She had told George that she could live with him having an affair. It was Leah who wouldn't keep it that way. She was the one who marched into Colleen's office and said flat out that she had been sleeping with George for two years.

"Didn't he tell you he was married?" Colleen asked her. "I mean, he wears a wedding ring. That must have given you some clue."

Leah's size, her smallness, her purse, her nails, her white sandals with the matching white bracelet were miniature. It had all made Colleen feel clumsy and old. She hadn't worn things that matched since she was a teenager.

"I've always known he was married," Leah told her. "It was one of the first things he told me about himself."

"You still went out with him?"

Leah nodded. She was the sort of woman whose face never expressed doubt. Her hair had been darker then. It was only November.

"When?" Colleen asked. George never went out of town. He never spent the night away from home. Most nights he was home by six-thirty, except on Tuesdays and Thursdays, when he worked out at a gym downtown. "When did you sleep with George?"

Leah shrugged and pursed her lips tight, keeping that part of the secret private. Colleen was so sure of the pattern in George's day that she suspected Leah of lying.

"You say you've been sleeping with him, so tell me when. Tell me so I'll know," Colleen said.

Leah sat quiet. She turned her head slightly and focused on the books to the left of the desk. Her hands were folded in her lap.

"You little liar!" Colleen stood up. "If you have something to tell me, then tell me. Don't sit here smirking at me. Tell me when George slept with you."

"Lunch time." Leah let the words loose. She got up quickly and lunged at the desk. Colleen imagined she was going to throw something at her. Instead Leah picked up Colleen's nameplate and thrust it in her face.

"This is going to end," Leah said. She dropped the nameplate in Colleen's lap and marched to the door. With her tiny hand on the knob she said, "It's going to end soon."

It wasn't until later that Colleen understood. Leah had been talking about her name. That was what was going to end. Leah was going to end her marriage.

"Do you think she's pretty?" Colleen asked Tricia. She scooped an ice cube from the water glass and ran it along her hairline. Sweating, she could smell the flower scent of her deodorant.

"You've asked me that a thousand times," Tricia said. She didn't look up from the menu.

"I promise this is the last time. I'll never mention her again," Colleen said. "Tell me what you think of her."

"She's okay," Tricia said. "Nothing special."

"You're just saying that," Colleen said. "She's beautiful. Really beautiful."

Colleen wanted Leah to be beautiful. Beauty would justify George leaving her. Even though no one would ever tell her Leah was beautiful, she continued to believe it.

"Why don't we leave?" Tricia said. She closed the menu and pushed her chair from the table. "You're just going to sit there and let Leah ruin your lunch."

"She's ruined my life. I don't see why I should care about this lunch."

"Why do you say things like that?"

"Because they're true."

"Colleen. Don't do this to me," Tricia said. "You make me feel so helpless."

"I'm horrible to be around," Colleen said. "I know I am. I can't help it."

"We can leave if it'd be easier," Tricia offered. She reached for her purse and got out her car keys.

"I promise. No more talk about Leah," Colleen said. "We can't leave. They have the most fantastic strawberry cheesecake here."

"I can't afford to eat sweets," Tricia said. She looked down and patted her stomach. "But you sure can. How much weight have you lost since Christmas?"

"I haven't kept track," Colleen said.

"When was the last time you were at this weight?"

"When I was fifteen."

"You look good," Tricia said.

"But not good enough." Colleen could hear the whine in

her voice. She tried to keep it quiet, to keep it inside, to keep it something small. She put her hand over her eyes so the waiter wouldn't see her crying. Tricia ordered lunch for both of them. It had always been easy to embarrass Tricia. Tricia cared about what people thought, even strangers. When they were young, Tricia had smacked into the corner of the coffee table and a black and blue mark colored her eye the next morning. She refused to leave the house, afraid someone would make fun of her—she spent the next two weeks of July in her bedroom, with no air conditioning, the wood dresser swelling with the heat, until the bruise faded.

The waiter moved away from the table. Colleen, with her head still down, blew her nose in the napkin. The material was rough and when she brought it up to her face she could smell the detergent it was washed in.

"Is that okay for lunch?" Tricia asked. "I can't remember if you eat turkey salad."

"It's fine."

"Ranch dressing?"

"It's perfect," Colleen said. "I'm sorry I'm acting this way. I can't help it. It just happens."

"Isn't it getting any better?" Tricia hunched slightly forward as if Colleen might tell her a secret. "Haven't you stopped thinking of them just a little?"

"Some," Colleen admitted. "At work I'm okay. That's getting better."

Even after George had confirmed his affair with Leah, Colleen kept it quiet at work. Some days she spent eight hours alone in her office drawing circles on the company letterhead. When her secretary finally asked her about the trash cans full of scribblings, Colleen told her, knowing she would tell the rest of the office. The secretary smiled when Colleen admitted that George was filing for divorce. She told Colleen they had all thought she had cancer. They were relieved to find it was only the end of her marriage.

"Does George still call you?" Tricia asked.

"No. He hasn't called in a month," Colleen said. "All he wanted then was to know what happened to his skis."

"Did you have them?"

"No. I sold them at the last garage sale."

"Good for you."

"I ran into his brother a couple of weeks ago," Colleen said. "He keeps me informed."

"What does he say?" Tricia held out the breadbasket, putting a seeded muffin on the side plate near Colleen's elbow when she shrugged it away.

"He told me George isn't really in love with Leah," Colleen said. She sipped at her wine and looked across the room where she could see the top of Leah's head. "George is attracted to her sexually. That's what he likes about her. He said she's different than anyone he's ever known."

"What does that mean? Is she different in bed?" Tricia asked.

"He didn't say and I wasn't about to ask. I guess she's talented. That she's got something I didn't have."

"Why would his brother tell you something like that?"

"He likes to make me feel bad," Colleen said. "I never was one of his favorites."

"But doesn't it make you feel better?" Tricia asked. "Now you can stop blaming yourself for everything. George must be a real weirdo if he married someone he doesn't even love. He's the one who has to spend the rest of his life with her."

"If it lasts," Colleen said. "Who ever said it was going to last?"

Colleen had gone to George's and Leah's wedding. She went alone, vowing never to tell anyone about it. She got to the church an hour before the ceremony and parked at the end of the lot. She angled the car in so the driver's side was up against a pile of snow and hung dry cleaning bags in the passenger window. By tilting the bottom of the hanger an inch, she could see the church without being seen. She had filled a thermos with orange juice and vodka and sipped at it, pleased with herself. It wasn't until she saw the bridesmaids, their rose gowns billowing beneath heavy winter coats, that she realized she had lost all control. She was the spectator now.

George's family arrived next. His mother looked older. Even from a distance, Colleen could see the slumping of her shoulders and the gray streaks in her dark hair. His father looked the same, maybe more of a belly than at her wedding. The brothers had grown up. No longer pimply teenagers, they were handsome in their identical tuxedos.

Colleen drank from the thermos. She missed Leah going into the church and wondered if there was a back room. It would be like Leah to sneak into the service. The wedding lasted half an hour. Colleen's feet, in boots without socks, were frozen. George and Leah walked down the steps through the arch of people to their car, a limousine with no paper flowers. Colleen got out of the car and waved. George stopped when he saw her. Colleen continued to wave as he pushed Leah into the car.

When George got back from his honeymoon, he called to ask why she had been at the wedding. "Were you drunk?" he asked.

"Why do you say that?" Colleen asked.

"Because whenever you do something stupid you're drunk," George said. She knew he was talking about the time she came to his apartment after drinking a whole bottle of Chablis. She knew he was asleep in the same bed with Leah and rang the doorbell fifty times. When they didn't answer, she went down to the shed and got a rake, which she pounded through the living room screen. George called the police, who drove her home. Tricia had to go back the next morning for her car.

"I don't even know who told you about the wedding," George said. "Do you know you made a fool out of yourself in front of everyone in my family? Don't you have any respect for yourself?"

Colleen was too ashamed to say anything in her defense.

Every time she thought about what she must have looked like, she was disgusted with herself. After George hung up, Colleen got busy and called a client. While she was waiting for the woman to come to the phone, she saw the whole scene at the wedding. It made her gag that she had been so desperate to go to the church. She hung up before the client got on the line.

"That's her mother," Colleen said. She had been staring across the room at Leah's table. "Leah's here with her mother."

"What?" Tricia started to turn around.

"No, don't look now," Colleen said. "She's looking this way."

"How do you know what her mother looks like?"

"I can tell. She looks just like Leah, except her hair is gray," Colleen said. She remembered seeing the woman at the wedding. One of the first people out of the church—she had been crying too.

"I thought we weren't going to talk about Leah," Tricia said. She spooned salad dressing onto her plate, covering the tomatoes with creamy sauce. "Colleen. Will you eat something?"

"I am," Colleen said. She cut up the lettuce and picked a small square off the end of her fork. "I'll be right back."

"Where are you going?"

"The bathroom," Colleen said.

"Why don't you wait?" Tricia asked. She turned to look at Leah's table.

"I'll go the long way around. They won't see me."

Tricia shook her head.

"Honest. I'll be right back."

Colleen stopped at the bar and borrowed a pen from the bartender. She wrote a short message on a cocktail napkin: "YOUR DAUGHTER RUINED MY LIFE." She folded the napkin twice and brought it up to the host stand. "Will you give this to the older woman at the table over there?" Colleen asked the hostess.

The girl smiled and looked out across the dining room. "Which table?"

Colleen looked around the wall. "Right over there. The two women. One's a fake blonde."

"Sure. I'd be glad to." The girl took the note and stuck it under the light on the host stand.

"It's important," Colleen said.

"I won't forget." The girl went back to wiping the plastic-coated menus with a damp rag.

Colleen went in the bathroom and stood in front of the mirror, shaking. She turned the faucet on cold and let the water run. Bending at the waist, she flipped her hair back and combed it down with her fingers.

Tricia came in and stood behind her. "What are you doing?"

"Nothing," Colleen said. "I was just coming out."

"I saw you talking to the hostess. Is anything wrong?"

"I don't feel good," Colleen said. She reached in her purse and pulled out her wallet. "Will you pay the bill? I'll meet you out at your car."

"What's wrong?" Tricia asked. "Did you get sick?"

"Not yet," Colleen said. "But I think I could. Maybe it's from having wine on a coffee stomach."

Tricia held Colleen's wrist when she handed her the wallet. "Your pulse is racing," she said. "Are you sure you're all right?"

"Fine," Colleen said.

"It's probably seeing Leah that's got you all upset," Tricia said.

Colleen's cheeks and throat were splotched with uneven red marks. It sometimes happened when she was nervous. She put the back of her hand against her face to feel the heat from her skin.

Leah always got what she wanted. In January George had promised Colleen he would come over to the house and shovel the driveway. She wanted him to get rid of all his junk in the garage too. She told him she couldn't list the house with so much of his stuff in the way. He was supposed to be there at 6 o'clock. At 5:45 Colleen drank a glass of white wine so she would be relaxed, not bitchy, maybe a little flushed when he got there. At 10:30 he called.

"I'm at the hospital," he said. "Leah cut her finger. I had to take her down to the emergency room."

"You're not coming?"

"Leah's kind of upset," George said.

"You were supposed to be here at 6," Colleen said.

"I know. It was a bad cut. She was cutting vegetables and sliced off the end of her finger."

"You're not coming?"

"It's late."

"I know what time it is."

"Listen. I had to go. Leah was scared. There was a lot of blood." George covered the phone. Although Colleen could feel the vibration of his voice, she couldn't tell what he was saying. She wanted to tell him that she never wanted him to mention Leah's name to her again, but instead she stuck to talking about the house.

"I want to get rid of this house," Colleen said. "I want to sell it as quickly as possible so I'll never have to think of you again. I can't sell it with all your crap still here."

"I can take the day off work tomorrow."

"You're not coming here when I'm not here."

"This is ridiculous," George said. "It's still my house too."

"Not anymore," Colleen said. "You moved out."

"I have a key. I'll be there tomorrow and get rid of everything. You can start showing the house by this weekend."

"No."

"Don't be difficult," George said. "This situation is hard on everybody."

But Colleen didn't see anyone suffering but herself. "I don't want you in this house when I'm not here," she said.

"Just ridiculous," George said. He spoke away from the phone and Colleen knew Leah was standing right next to him.

George would tell her everything Colleen had said, and she was ashamed.

Colleen walked out to Tricia's car. She wiped the dirt from the chrome around the window. The sun was hot. She squinted, looking back at Archibald's Restaurant. She recognized Leah's short determined walk coming at her.

"Who do you think you are?" Leah shouted.

Colleen picked at the dust trapped under her fingernails.

"Where do you get off writing my mother notes like that?" Leah shouted. She stood right in front of Colleen. "Who do you think you are?"

It was difficult to look at Leah. Colleen didn't want to be this close to her.

"Can't you leave us alone?" Leah said. Her breath was short and she spoke as if it gave her great pains to say anything. "Are you listening to me?"

Colleen could not look at Leah and instead stared at the tires.

"Leave us alone," Leah said. "We're finished with you."

"You want me to leave you alone?" Colleen asked.

"You're not married to George anymore. Doesn't that sink in?" Leah said. "Stay out of our lives."

Tricia came up and stood beside Colleen. Her keys jangled from the heavy chain. "Get in the car, Colleen," Tricia said. She unlocked the door. Colleen didn't move. Tricia tried to force the door open. It hit Colleen at the hip, but she stood firm.

"You want me to leave you alone?" Colleen shouted. "What about me? That's what I've been asking all along. I wanted you to leave me alone. I wanted you out of my life."

"George and I are married now," Leah said.

"So what?" Colleen asked. She looked away from Leah, talking to no one, but arguing things she had argued with herself since the start. "I was married to him the whole time you were sleeping with him."

"He loves me."

"You did ruin my life. You were sleeping with a married man and you couldn't have cared less," Colleen said. "Do you know what you did to my life? I don't even have any memories. Every time I look at my photographs I have to remind myself that you were sleeping with him."

"Get in the car," Tricia said. She took hold of Colleen's arm and forced her to move over so she could get the door open.

"George hates you," Leah said. "I know that for a fact. He couldn't wait to divorce you."

"That doesn't mean he loves you."

"He despises you."

"And he sleeps around on you," Colleen said. "Just like he did on me."

Tricia threw her arms around Colleen and pulled her closer to the car.

"George told me the happiest day of his life was the day he moved out of your house," Leah yelled.

Tricia let go of Colleen and turned to Leah. "Get out of here," she said.

Colleen held onto the car and stared at her sister.

"She started it," Leah said. "She's the one who's jealous. She wrote my mother that note."

"You got everything you wanted, didn't you?" Tricia yelled. "Didn't you get everything you wanted? Yes, you did. Yes, you did." She took slow steps forward, making Leah back up. Colleen could see the sweat on the back of her knees running down her calves.

"I'm not doing anything. She's the one that keeps bothering us," Leah said. "She calls in the middle of the night and then hangs up."

"Go away," Tricia said. She kept moving forward.

"She can't get anyone else—that's why she keeps bothering George," Leah said. "She's trying to hang onto him."

Tricia slapped her—quickly and forcefully right across the face. She turned away and told Colleen to get in the car. Colleen stared at Leah.

"Get in the car now," Tricia commanded Colleen.

Colleen slammed the door and bent forward, surrounding herself with the interior of the car. The seat burned her legs through her nylons. Tricia fumbled with the keys, dropping them when she tried to fit one into the ignition. She pulled away from the curb into traffic. Colleen sat up and looked back into the side mirror to see if Leah was still on the sidewalk. The sun hit the chrome, making it impossible to see anything but an intense glare. She turned to Tricia, who was driving with tears running down her face.

"You hit Leah," Colleen said. "You just slapped her."

"I know," Tricia said. She made no move to get rid of the tears. Colleen pulled open the door of the glove compartment and got out a tissue. She handed it to Tricia. But Tricia kept her hands on the wheel. Colleen leaned over and wiped her sister's face. She started to laugh.

"I can't believe you just hit Leah," she said. "I don't believe it."

Tricia turned off the main road to a side street and pulled over to the curb. She took the tissue from Colleen and blew her nose.

"That felt great," Colleen said.

"It really did," Tricia pulled the rearview mirror so she could see her face. With the edge of her fingernail she wiped off the thin streak of mascara running alongside her nose.

"It felt wonderful." Colleen laughed. "Just wonderful."

"I'd do it again," Tricia said. "In a flash, if you needed me to."

"You should have seen how shocked Leah was," Colleen said. "She just couldn't believe it. I couldn't believe it."

"Someone had to help you," Tricia said. "You never would have done it."

"No. I wouldn't have." Colleen laughed. "I never would have done it like that."

They sat in the car for a few more minutes until Colleen looked at her watch and realized how long she had been away from the office. Tricia cleaned her face again and then they pulled back on the main road, back into the moving traffic.

The Lady on the Plane

I sat next to a lady from Logan to Metro who told me it made her sick to read in flight. She ordered coffee with three packs of sugar and balanced the cup on the cardboard box in her lap.

"Let me stick that down here for you," I said. I uncrossed my legs to show her the empty space under the seat in front of me.

"No, thank you," she said. "This is fine." She was extremely beautiful. Her thick hair was pulled away from her face and fastened in a silver clip at the nape of her neck. The flight had originated in Dublin and her pale skin was marred by a red circle in the center of her cheek where she must have slept against something rough. It was a night flight, but the plane smelled of early morning—brewed coffee and an odd odor of stale chocolate.

"Are you sure?" I asked. "There's plenty of room down here."

"It's very valuable," she said. "I'm afraid someone will kick it."

Her earlobe started to bleed and she handed me her cup. She had sipped the coffee in a haphazard fashion, kissing the plastic at different places each time, and the rim was stained with thick orangey lines. My finger was too fat to fit in the handle and the coffee burned through the plastic.

"Can I get you something?" I asked.

"What about a Band-Aid?" She shrugged when she said it, as if a Band-Aid would be the last thing a man like me, someone wearing a full suit, the tie not loosened, would carry. "Don't worry. It's been bleeding since we left Dublin."

"Is it the altitude?" The coffee spilled on my pants as the plane lowered into slight turbulence. I rubbed it in with my knuckles. The small diamond on my wedding band caught a string and snagged the material.

"That could be," she said. "It's very dry in here."

"It'll be better when we land," I promised. I liked the formal tone to our conversation and undid my seat belt. Most of the other passengers slept and I welcomed their silence. A business trip in Boston had been cut short by a hysterical phone call from my wife, who told me her nineteen-year-old brother had been missing for ten days. He had disappeared without telling anyone—not his boss at the racquet club, not his girlfriend of four months. My wife's mother, who at first thought it was nothing, was now frantic. She had contacted the police.

"Do you think they'll show a movie?" the woman asked.

"No," I said. "The flight is too short."

The tissue was pressed into her ear and she asked me to repeat my reply.

"Three hours should be enough time for a movie," she said.

"It won't take us that long to get to Detroit." I sipped her coffee; the lipstick tasted of a perfume I knew. The summer before I got married, I dated a girl on Martha's Vineyard who wore it to the beach in the afternoon sun. It's called Opium and like the drug is dangerous. My wife thinks it smells like crowded department stores.

"I'm flying to Minneapolis," the woman said. "We're scheduled to arrive at midnight." She wore a black skirt and when she crossed her legs I could see the thin white lace of her slip.

"I didn't know it was a continuing flight," I said. Her nylons were gray, but sheer, and the muscles in her legs were well defined.

The woman sighed and shifted the box on her lap. The mailing label had been sliced and the letters USA were written in blue magic marker on the side flap. The rest of the address was in ink; the lines looped and curled like words, but I couldn't read them. The woman followed my gaze into her lap.

"Didn't my father have horrible handwriting?" she said. "He used to send me letters and cards all the time, but I couldn't read them."

"Did he write that?" I asked.

She ignored my question. "He worked in a butcher shop. In

Dublin. It's like a deli here in the States. He did all the books and no one could read a word he wrote. I bought him a type-writer. Just a small one for his desk, but he wouldn't use it. He said he never had a problem reading his own handwriting. The people who delivered the meat used to kid him and tell him they couldn't read their checks and he used to say if they couldn't read them, maybe they shouldn't cash them."

She shivered and tugged again at her skirt. I asked if she wanted to use my overcoat for a blanket, but she said she was fine.

"I think this is addressed to my mother. She lives with us in Minneapolis." The woman traced the circular handwriting with the tip of her fingernail. "He's only been dead ten days."

"My God," I said. "I'm so sorry to hear that." I felt that it was right to reach for her hand. She didn't flinch when I touched her. "I'm very sorry."

"I flew over as soon as we heard he was sick," the woman said. "I went alone. My mother's terrified to fly and my hus-band had to stay with the kids."

I finished her coffee. It had turned cold and a few coffee flakes at the bottom caught in my throat. I coughed and shook my head. "Very, very sorry," I said. I pushed the cup down inside the seat pocket next to the in-flight magazine.

"My father should have been with us here in the States, but he was too stubborn to leave Ireland. I told him he was going to die alone," the woman said. "But that didn't scare him. He wouldn't have left that house for anything. Not for anything in the world. Wild horses couldn't have dragged him from that house."

We turned our heads to the aisle as the stewardess walked by with a tray of hot towels. They were rolled into long cylin-ders and she used a pair of tongs to pass them around. Very few customers were awake to take them.

"People get used to their ways," I told the woman. I thought about my own home. My wife had been complaining constantly about a new place, but I couldn't find a reason to leave; the yard is more than an acre and in the summer two kids down the block cut the lawn for fifteen dollars. I've become familiar with the sounds of our street. My wife argues that the school system is poor, but she says she doesn't want to have kids just yet.

"My father was a very obsessive man," the woman said. "He grew up in the house he died in. He spent his whole life in that one house. My mother and I used to pray that someone would come by and tear the house down. That would have been his only salvation."

"Was he happy there?" I asked.

"Happy? My father, happy?" The woman laughed. I smiled with her although I wasn't sure why her mood had changed.

"Maybe he was afraid to leave his home." I suddenly felt very close to this man and his daughter who didn't understand him. "He probably saw his home as his security."

"He was totally obsessed with his photographs. He wouldn't leave the house because of the photographs," she said. "You've never seen anything like it in your life."

"Photographs?" I asked. "What photographs?"

The stewardess stood at the row in front of us. She was so close I could see white threads scattered on the dark material of her uniform. The plane suddenly lurched and she stumbled backward. The tray tipped and the towels fell to the floor. I grabbed her elbow and held her with both hands until the plane settled a bit.

The woman next to me asked me to pick up one of the towels. Her earlobe had started bleeding again. I handed her two. She seemed unaware that we might be in some danger.

"My father took a photograph of himself every day," she said. "Every day of his life."

"Are you kidding?" I asked. The stewardess stood up and reached for the handle of the overhead compartment to hold her balance.

"There are hundreds of photographs," the woman continued. "No. More than that. Thousands of photographs. All of
himself. He had cabinet files full of photographs. All from
the same place. In that same chair. That's why it took me so
long to pack his things. It wasn't the clothes or getting rid
of the furniture, but I had to ship all his photographs to
Minneapolis."

"That's amazing," I said. The man across the aisle from me
woke up and immediately lit a cigarette. I usually don't like the
smell, but when the smoke drifted overhead, I breathed in
deeply and thought of mint leaves in the summer. My wife's
brother smokes constantly. It is one of the many things we
disagree about. When we are together there is always tension.

The woman next to me tucked the hot towel in the collar of
her blouse and continued. "It began as a hobby," she said. "My
grandparents thought it was cute. He was only eight years old
when he started so it didn't seem like there was anything
wrong. When all the other kids came home from school and
changed into their play clothes, my father would put on his
Sunday suit. Then he'd set up his place in the foyer. He sat in
a dining room chair right near the front window. He took the
photographs in the same place every day."

The woman's eyes were slightly puffy. She looked like the
kind of woman who never cried in public and for a moment I
debated asking her why she was afraid to let people see her in
tears. My wife cries at odd times, and it makes me feel powerful to be able to comfort her. It is the one way I feel I can
protect her.

"He liked the view from there," she said. "The sun was usually setting and the shadows were interesting to look at."

The stewardess walked forward, using each seat to steady
her movements. I watched her disappear into the cabin. The
No Smoking sign flashed on.

"He just kept on taking photographs of himself. Every day.
All through grade school and even when he got into high

school. His parents begged him to apply to the university, but he didn't want to leave the house. The day he finished school he went straight into my uncle's butcher shop."

"Was that so bad?" I asked.

"He worked in the butcher shop until it closed five years ago," she said. "That was his life. Forty-five years in the butcher shop and sixty years of photographs. He couldn't stop taking his photographs."

"Why didn't he bring the camera with him when he left town?" I looked down at my watch: twenty minutes to twelve. I tried to think of something reassuring to tell my wife if there still was no news of her brother. I wasn't worried about his disappearance. He is a brash kid whose ego always gets in his way. Once, at a Super Bowl Sunday party at our house, he threatened to blow my brains out if I ever refused his sister anything. It had come out of nowhere, a few hours of drinking beer. His sudden anger and drunkenness repulsed me and I told him to leave the house. Later, when I told my wife about it, she laughed. "He's being protective," she said. "He's my little brother. Couldn't you cut him some slack?"

"My father wouldn't leave the house," the woman said. "Location was everything. The photographs had to be taken in the same place every day. He loved the light there. The way it came in through the windows made long shadows on the floor. The shadows changed with the seasons."

A small bell rang overhead and I clutched at the armrests. The woman noticed my nervousness and made a series of small clicking noises with her tongue.

"Don't be nervous," she said. "Look." She opened the top flap of the box and pulled out a handful of black-and-white photographs. "I have my favorites here," she said. "Just look at them. Aren't they wonderful?" She handed me three photographs after shuffling through the group. "Just look at my father."

There was a sound of static, then the captain's voice announced that Detroit was under fog. He had thought we could make it in before the airport closed, he said, but the tower had just informed them that it was too dangerous to allow more planes to land. We would be flying back to Toledo.

I put the photographs on my lap and pulled my jacket sleeve back to look at my watch. My wife would be worried if I was late. I wondered how long we would be stuck in Toledo. I hoped she wasn't alone. I didn't want her to sit up waiting, although I knew she would—waiting at her place in the living room, cursing as every car drove past, the headlights flashing on the bay window and disappearing down the dark street.

"My father swears that this was the first photograph he took," the woman said. "See how young he was then."

She began flipping through the photographs. The diamond-cut edges on some had yellowed; at first glance, many of them seemed identical. I looked at them closely as she passed them to me—the window behind the man's head, the various degrees of light, his direct stare into the camera eye. He sat posed in a dark suit. His hair, light as a boy, had darkened as a young man and then started to disappear—his forehead looked larger and larger as he aged. The woman dug into the cardboard box and pulled out more. She handed me a batch tied with green ribbon.

"These are some that I watched him take," she said. "I was young, about four or five, and he would let me look into the camera while he waited for it to click."

The man sat in these with the same look on his face, oblivious that someone else was in the room with him.

"See how much he's changed in these?" the woman asked. "You can tell he knew he had responsibilities. He had three kids at that time and two babies dead. The one he took the day the twins died is so sad. They were only three days old. I had to pack it away. I couldn't look at it."

In all the photographs the man wore a tie, the same dark color as the suit.

"My mother's anxious to see the photographs," the woman continued. "She wants to see if he was any different after she left him."

She leaned over and whispered in my ear. "We're burying him in Minneapolis. My mother insisted, because she's too afraid to fly and it would take too long for her to travel over by boat."

"I understand," I said. She kept handing me photographs and I looked at all of them.

"His body is on the plane," she said. "Below us." She pointed down. "In baggage." She covered her eyes with the damp towel.

I couldn't think of anything to say to her. I shook my head and looked back to the photographs. There was a slight resemblance between the woman and her father. They shared angular jaws and long necks. I told her I thought she looked like her father.

"Do you think so?" the woman asked. She lifted the towel from her eyes and dropped it to the floor. "No one has ever told me that. I hope it's true."

"It's true," I said. I was disappointed she was not crying; I would have liked an opportunity to hold her, to comfort her. Instead I held one photograph up next to her face and looked back and forth between the two. They were very much alike. They shared the man's seriousness.

"I always thought I looked like my father," she said. "But everyone told me I was the image of my mother."

The plane was descending quickly. My ears filled with pressure and it was hard to hear the woman over the roar in my eardrums. I pinched my nose, trying to blow the pressure out. I felt like a scuba diver, holding my breath as if it was necessary to make it to the surface. The woman handed me a photograph of her father when he was a teenager. His legs touched the floor and his shoulders had begun to round forward.

"Do you think I look like him here?" she asked.

"Yes," I said. "Very much so."

The stewardess walked by quickly. The plane was at an odd angle and it took her a long time to make it to the front of the plane. I watched as she slid into the drop seat and buckled herself in. There were too many photographs on my lap and I could not redo my seatbelt. The lights on the ground were moving in closer. I began to put the photographs back in the box.

"Let me take one more look," she said. "I'm so glad you think I look like him."

The plane turned sharply and I could see the green lights lining the runway. I braced my feet against the metal bar under the seat in front of me and tried to brake the speed. The moment the wheels touched the ground, the compartments overhead dropped open and the white oxygen masks jumped out. Suspended by thick cords, they swung back and forth. There was a second of screaming before the passengers caught the masks and pulled them to their mouths. My mask landed right on my face and I held it in place with both hands. I began breathing very fast, trying to save up oxygen. The woman next to me shook her head.

"We're not in danger," she said. "We're already on the ground."

The stewardess stood in the aisle and cupped her hands over her mouth like a megaphone. "Don't panic," she shouted. "We are not losing oxygen. You can breathe without them."

I turned to the window and saw that we were taxiing in toward the airport terminal. I let go of my mask and it swung forward. I yanked it down and dropped it to the floor.

"I'm sorry," I said. I was embarrassed and folded my hands in my lap.

"There's nothing to be afraid of," she said calmly. "I made the plane foolproof. It would be too tragic if something happened to the plane with me on board."

She straightened the photographs and placed them back in

the box. She folded the flaps closed and then put her hand over mine on the armrest.

The captain announced that it would be at least another hour before they would know if Metro was going to reopen. He went on to say that it was possible for Detroit-bound passengers to deplane in Toledo—the car rental agency would be open and the Greyhound bus was running. I wanted to wait on the plane next to the woman, but she turned to me and spoke quietly.

"Thank you for looking at my photographs," she said. "I've enjoyed talking to you."

I got up and buttoned my raincoat. "The photographs are very nice," I said.

"I'll think of you," she said. "When I remember this horrible trip."

I nodded and reached for my briefcase in the overhead compartment.

"Be careful if you drive," she continued. "The roads are always bad in the fog."

I leaned down across the seat and kissed the woman on her lips, the orange lipstick now faded. She held my hand for a moment, not surprised that I had kissed her. We said good-bye at the same time and I moved down the aisle to the open door.

The Toledo Airport was empty. The signs behind the ticket counters were blank—no posted cities or departure times. Our small group from the plane walked down the nonmoving escalator, following the signs directing us to the baggage claim area. The others talked about the flight. Two of the men had come from Dublin and were exhausted. Downstairs, a man in a green uniform crossed the terminal to the car rental place and we stood in line on the other side of the counter. He tried to arrange car pools, but I was the only one headed for a northern suburb. When it was my turn, I handed him my charge card and he typed some things into the computer and had me sign three forms. He handed me the car keys and told me he would call a shuttle to take me out to the parking lot. I told him I wanted to walk, that I needed to stretch my legs before the drive home.

The night air was filled with rain; halfway across the parking lot, I remembered that I had forgotten to call my wife. My socks were damp and I did not want to walk back to the terminal. I told myself I would stop at a gas station once I got to I-75.

The road got worse as I drove north. The fog drifted across the highway from the Detroit River and at one point became so dense that I had to pull off to the shoulder. I waited with the radio on full volume. The fog swept around me in a slow continuous motion. To the right, the air cleared and I could see one of the downriver power plants towering on the other side of a fence. The sudden appearance of the dark structure scared me and I accelerated back onto the highway in total darkness. A truck's taillights came into view and I moved in closer. The large tires filtered a steady spray against my windshield. I turned the wipers up higher.

I didn't notice the fog lifting; but as I put miles behind me, I began to recognize certain landmarks: the Canada Dry billboard, the Uniroyal tire. The truck led me through the downtown bypass before turning off toward Port Huron. I headed north—the only other car on the highway. The radio was becoming repetitive and I turned it off, but the sudden silence bothered me more so I flicked it back on.

I could see the living room lights spilling out on the front lawn from halfway down the block. My wife was sitting at the kitchen table with a coffee cup. There were red circles on the table and I knew she was drinking wine. I went over and hugged her.

"Is there any news?" I asked.

Her face was very pale, void of any color. It reminded me of the fog, of dangers not apparent on the surface.

"Nothing," she said. "Nothing at all."

"I'm sorry," I said. "Can I do anything?"

"It's late," my wife said. She moved away from the table and looked up at the clock over the stove. "Did you miss your plane?"

"No," I said. "It was the fog. We had to land in Toledo."

There was a noise from the other room and I looked over the counter into the living room.

"That's mother," my wife said. "I told her she could stay with us."

"Of course," I said. "Should we help her into bed?"

"No," she said. "She was afraid to be alone. Let her sleep there. I don't want to wake her."

"How is she doing?" I whispered.

Her face was turned into the couch, but I could hear her sharp, deep breathing. The green and white afghan from the rocking chair was pulled up to her shoulders. Her head was resting on the two small end pillows. They were a Christmas gift from someone at the office, with seven apples embroidered in a circle around a dark brown oak. The stitching had frayed from use and the red yarn in the apples had faded.

"Not very well," my wife said. She drank from the cup and asked if I wanted anything.

"I'm fine," I said.

"Did you eat on the plane?"

"Yes," I said. "No. I had a sandwich in Boston."

I took off my suit coat and followed my wife to the back of the house. I stopped in the living room to turn off the lamp on the table behind the couch and my wife took my hand.

"Leave it on," she said. "I don't want her to wake up in the dark."

My wife carried her cup into the bedroom, finishing the wine before sitting on the bed. She kicked off her shoes and massaged her toes with her fingers. I put my suit coat on a hanger; when I hung it in the closet, I saw something sticking out of the side pocket. I reached in and was startled to see three of the photographs from the woman on the plane. The old man in his pose by the window was out of place in my house. I didn't remember putting them in my pocket and I wondered if I could have done it when the oxygen masks were released. I didn't know how I would get them back to the lady on the plane. I turned to my wife, who had stretched out on the bed. From the way her shoulders moved on the pillow, I could tell she was crying.

"I'm sorry." I sat beside her. "I'm really sorry. Is there anything I can do for you?"

"I'm scared," she said.

"Don't be," I whispered. I rubbed her back. Her shoulder muscles stiffened when I touched her.

"I'm so worried," she said. "Mom is going crazy with worry."

"Everything is going to be fine," I said. "You'll see. It's going to be fine."

She lifted her face from the pillow, her eyes closed. "Do you think so?" she asked. "Do you think he's all right?"

"Yes," I said. "You'll see." I bent down to kiss her. I could taste the sweet wine on her lips. She cried harder and I hugged her, moving my fingers through her hair. The curtains were pulled and the room was lit only with the light from the closet.

"Do you think you could sleep?" I asked.

"Are you coming to bed?"

"In a minute," I said. "I'll check to make sure the house is locked up."

She rolled over onto her stomach and turned her face to the wall.

"Don't you want to change?" I said. "Why don't you get under the covers?"

"I'll wait for you," she said.

I went into the hallway and turned up the heat. I walked around the house, checking the heating ducts to make sure every room was warm. I didn't want anyone waking up cold. The furniture cast familiar shadows on the walls as I moved silently through each room. I was in the kitchen when the telephone rang. I picked up the receiver quickly.

I talked to the state police in the dark, a draft blowing up from the floorboards.

The neighbor's bedroom light flicked on. A moment later, it went out and the night was black again. The policeman told me they had found my brother-in-law's car two miles from the interstate in northern Wisconsin. It looked like suicide, but nothing was certain. They needed someone from the family to make a positive identification of the body. His wallet, the policeman told me, was found in his back pocket.

"I'll be down," I said. "Let me tell my wife first."

"That's fine," he said. He was very polite. "I'm very sorry."

"Yes," I said. "Thank you."

I put the phone back on the hook and watched the neighbor's house for any more flashes of light. It remained quiet. My mother-in-law's breathing was still heavy with worry—she had not been interrupted by the phone. She sometimes woke near morning for water. I filled a glass and left it on the coffee table near her head. I hoped she would see it before getting up. I slid the dead bolt across the front door and went back to the bedroom.

My wife was asleep. Her arms were tucked under her chest and when I touched her hand she did not stir. She slept on top of the blanket and I did not want to move it to cover her. I went to the closet for my suit coat. The sleeves were damp from the rain in Toledo. I removed the photographs from the pocket and covered my wife. Her legs were curled under and her small frame almost fit in the coat. I pushed her hair away from her face and the heat from her breath touched my fingers.

I hid the photographs in a book in the bottom drawer of my dresser. The wood moaned as I slid the drawer shut. I couldn't wake my wife and I didn't want to leave her alone in case she woke when I was gone. I pulled the chair over to the window, telling myself I would wait an hour before leaving. I watched my wife. Her face, deep in sleep, was calm. The lines around her eyes and mouth were relaxed and I dreaded waking her. I waited another hour. Outside, on the front porch, I heard the newspaper land on the step. I moved the curtain to one side and saw the neighbor boy riding his bike down the sidewalk. He tossed the papers mechanically at each house as he pedaled to the corner. My wife slept. The early morning light came through the window in thin rays across the carpet and I stayed still as if I had the power to hold that frame.

Independence Day

The Fourth of July pig roast at Lannie's was the first party I've been to since John died. I prefer to stay in the house. There's so much work to do here and I don't like to be away for long. The kids went to summer camp the first of June and I spent the month in the attic going through the cardboard boxes and musty trunks that have been up there for years. The days were hot and the sun poured through the roof, raising the temperature past 100 degrees. But when I look at how much I got done without throwing anything out, I feel that I'm accomplishing things. We live in John's great-aunt's house, which has been in the family for five generations, and it comforts me to look into the past. I plan to spend July in the basement. There is a wood paneled television set that's in good condition and a 1940 Victrola that needs to be refinished. I only went to Lannie's party because her husband Richard called me every night for a week to make sure I hadn't changed my mind. I thought going was easier than arguing.

I was doing fine at the party until Tim called me a chicken. He picked up a sparkler from the lawn and held it to my face. "You're afraid of these, aren't you?" he asked. The flame had burned out and the end glowed intense red.

"Not at all," I said. I swatted his hand away and leaned back against the picnic table. The air was fresh and clean after a week of thunderstorms and the weeping willows cast long shadows on the grass. The kids played hide and go seek under the leafy vines.

"Yes, you are," he insisted. "I've been watching you. You flinch every time they light one." He ran the sparkler through his fingers and then touched it to my cheek. It was warm but did not burn. The embers flaked against my skin and I brushed them with the back of my hand.

"Shouldn't you be helping with the pig?" I asked. I took a short sip of my vodka and tonic. The ice had melted hours ago. Lannie made it for me the minute I walked into the kitchen. She is nervous when I'm around and avoids talking about John.

We talk about our kids or the upcoming bluegrass festival that she's in charge of.

Tim dropped the sparkler on the lawn and I thought he was done teasing me.

"I'm starving," I said to him. "When's that pig going to be ready?"

"They're just kids' toys," Tim said.

"But they're throwing them," I said. "Someone could get hurt."

"Don't be a ninny," Tim said. "How are they going to hurt someone?"

"They could burn someone's leg or arm or even their eye," I said. My voice caught in my throat and I took another sip of the watery drink. It did not taste good and I tossed it out on the grass.

"You're a chicken," Tim said again. He put his hands on my shoulders to show he was just having a good time with me, but I couldn't help it. I'm not superstitious—I don't believe any amount of tea leaves mixed in with a pinch of graham cracker crumbs would have saved John from Lake St. Clair—but ever since he died, I have been afraid of the lake and everything else. I wanted to let Tim know the truth.

"Yes," I said. "I guess I am." I got up and pushed his hands off my shoulders. The wood planks under my bare feet were hot and I winced. "I am a big chicken. One of these days I'm going to wake up with feathers and then no one will be able to talk to me."

I ran to the house and let the screen door slam behind me. The ceiling fan in the living room moved swiftly and the cool air circled the dark room. I felt better inside the house. A yellow color flashed in my eyes from the change in light and I stood still, trying to lose the dizziness.

Lannie's voice came from the kitchen.

"She brought something over, but I don't know what I'm going to do with it." Lannie's voice is unmistakably eastern.

Originally from Boston, she still adds Rs to certain words.

"Is it that bad?" I did not recognize the other woman's voice, but I knew they were talking about me.

"Look at it," Lannie said. "She must have used fourteen heads of cabbage to make it."

I could hear the rustle of the aluminum foil I had used to cover the bin of coleslaw.

"It's heavy," she said. "How did she ever carry it over?"

"It's frozen," Lannie said. "Frozen solid."

"Oh, the poor thing," the woman said. "How is she doing?"

"I thought she was getting better," Lannie said. "But I don't know. What should I do? Should I put it on the buffet table and try to pass the word not to take it?"

"She's going to notice if no one's serving themselves. How long has her husband been dead?"

"It's been a year," Lannie said. I heard the refrigerator door open and close and then the sound of water running in the sink. "Poor, poor thing," Lannie echoed.

I bypassed the kitchen and made my way up the stairs. I walked close to the wall so if anyone came in the front door they would not see me. I hurried to the end of the hall to Lannie's guest bedroom. The twin beds were covered with matching blue and white bedspreads and the pillowcases had ivory lace around the edges. I sat on the bed nearest the window. Outside, Lannie walked across the patio carrying bowls of salads, beans, and chips to the picnic table. She did not set out my coleslaw, but I knew she would tell everyone about it. Lannie is not mean, but she shows that she cares in strange ways. I had made the coleslaw over a month ago and then stuck it in the downstairs refrigerator only to forget about it until this morning when there was no time for it to thaw. Cleaning the house and rearranging all the boxes takes up most of my energy. The grocery store down the street makes me nervous—everyone knows about John. My next-door neighbor shops for me. She leaves the bags of groceries on the back steps. She wasn't home this morning or I would have asked her to buy something else that I could take to Lannie's.

Ever since John died, I have been afraid. At night I sleep close to one edge of the bed with my hands beneath my body. They fall asleep and when I wake up they are numb. I lie awake thinking I will never lose the tingling sensation—that it will spread throughout my body and soon my legs and arms and then my head will be numb as my hands. They hurt and I don't move them for fear of disturbing the pain. I can see the outline of the doorway and the hall light is always on—even since I took Marni and Joey to riding camp up north. I didn't want them here this summer. I can't get away from the scene in Lake St. Clair and I'm afraid to let my kids see how scared I am of the images I still see in my head. I have played the scene over and over again—rearranging time and events.

I can see the rim of the boat and feel the tilting, the unsteadiness of the waves. The water is getting dark and we watch the sun set behind the row of houses on the shoreline. Tim wants to know the time and I tell him it's just past nine. He says we will turn on the lights in half an hour—when the sun has completely disappeared. Out of nowhere, a strong wind catches the boat and turns us to one side. John is sitting up front, holding his balance with his feet hooked under the steel bar. Richard tries to grab him, but the wind is strong and takes us all by surprise. The night is getting black and the waves are like the ocean. We tack and turn around and tack and turn around again. The flare is broken and we start to lose sight of John. I scream for him, but Richard says to keep calm. There is no reason to worry. He tells Lannie to take me down into the cabin. But I refuse to stay there. The lake gets darker and darker and finally we don't know where to look anymore.

I hate remembering, but it never goes away.

Richard found me in the bedroom. He was in charge of roasting the pig and his overalls were greased with butter and barbecue sauce. He smelled of a campfire, smoky burnt wood. He sat next to me on the bed and followed my gaze out the window.

"What do you see out there?" he asked.

The paper lanterns tied to the clothesline cast uneven patterns of light on the lawn. People swarmed around the picnic table.

Richard reached over and wrapped his arms around me. I moved my head into his chest and my lip hit the snap of his overalls. I bit down on the sore and felt the blood rush to the surface. I closed my eyes. Richard has a harder time talking to me than anyone else does. It was his sailboat and he should have been able to get us around to rescue John. But he was drunk—an afternoon full of vodka and cranberry drinks—and he said everything was happening so fast, he just couldn't get it together. He won't tell me his nightmares, but sometimes when he is near, I can feel his pain and I know he blames himself for my sadness.

"What can we do for you, Katie?" he asked.

"Take me home," I said right away. "I'm tired. I left the cole-slaw in the downstairs refrigerator too long and it's stiff as can be. Lannie couldn't serve it."

"There's plenty of food," he said. "It's all set out. Why don't you eat something?"

"Tim called me a chicken," I said. A warm breeze came in the window; the leaves of the large oak brushed against the screen. Below, someone shouted something and they all turned their heads to the river. They laughed, the sound of their voices quickly filling the yard.

"He was just kidding around," Richard said. "Tim didn't mean to upset you."

I didn't say anything and Richard sighed.

"I wish I could help," he said.

The laughter started up again, louder this time. I wanted to be home. The walls of my house are sturdy and inside I feel safe. Besides, I had just started going through the kids' old clothes—winter parkas, T-shirts, knee socks—things they no longer wear.

"Will you drive me home?" I asked Richard.

"If that's what you want." He stood and reached for my hand. "Are you sure you want to leave?"

"Yes," I said. "I'm better off at home."

We sneaked out the front door and down the driveway to Richard's van. The sharp stones of the gravel reminded me that my sandals were under the picnic table. Richard volunteered to go back and get them, but I told him they weren't important. I didn't want him to tell Lannie he was taking me home. I knew she would try to convince me to stay for the fireworks.

Richard turned on the radio and we listened to three songs on the Top 40 countdown. Mosquitoes flew in the windows and danced on my bare legs.

"I'm getting air conditioning next summer for this thing," he said.

"Marni thinks we should air-condition the bedrooms," I said. "I don't really think we need it, but I want to make it as comfortable as possible for them."

"You should get out more, Katie," Richard said. We turned down the street and I saw the white of my porch light.

"I'm comfortable there," I said. "It's an old house and there's a lot of taking care that needs to be done."

"Lannie told me you sent your kids to camp up north for two months." He pulled up the driveway and shut off the motor.

"I had to," I said. "I thought they should be with other kids. You know, to have a chance to do things."

"I don't know," Richard said. "It's none of my business, but don't you think you could manage better if they were around?"

"I just want them to start having a good time," I said. "We've all been mourning for so long."

Richard opened his door and the mosquitoes flew to the overhead light. I got out and he walked me up to the front porch. We hugged good-bye and I went in the house. The radio in the living room was playing gospel music. I keep it on all the time. It doesn't matter to me if it's music or news.

I was in Marni's room, folding her baby dresses, when the phone rang. Her clock on the nightstand had stopped and I wasn't sure of the time. I rubbed the rough cotton against my cheek and picked up the phone. "Hello," I said.

It was the camp director up north. Joey had been having nightmares every night since he arrived. They had waited, she said, but now they were worried. Marni had slept in Joey's cabin two nights in a row and still he woke up screaming and crying for home.

"Is he there?" I asked. "Can I talk to him?"

Joey didn't say anything at first, but I could hear him crying.

"Joey?" I said. "Is that you? How are you, sweetheart?"

He sobbed into the receiver. "I want to come home."

"Put the phone down," I said. "Go get a drink of water. I'll be here."

He kept crying into the phone. He gets migraines when he cries and I knew that before morning he would throw up.

"Go on, honey," I said. The room was stuffy and I wiped a bead of sweat from my chest.

"Marni and I want to come home," he said. "We want to come home."

"Okay, baby," I said. "Don't worry." I cradled the phone between my chin and my shoulder and walked to the window. "Have you been swimming up there? What about Marni? Does she go riding?"

"I miss you," Joey said. "I want to come home."

The director got on and told me she wanted the kids to call me back in the morning. "I understand the situation," she said. "The nights are usually the hardest time. We'll see if they still want to come home in the morning."

"Tell them good night," I said. "Tell them I miss them. I love them."

After I hung up, I stayed at the window. The backyard was

dark. Mr. Schott, the neighbor to my right, called for his dog. His voice echoed in the empty yards and then I heard the screen door shut. I looked to the sky for clouds. I like it best when it rains. It's comforting to be inside when it's overcast. Something bright flashed near the window and I thought it might be lightning. I lifted the screen and held my palm to the sky to catch the first drops of rain. The light shimmered, sparkling red and then a short flash of blue. It kept changing colors. I ran downstairs and unlocked the back door.

The night was warm and the wind still. The dark sky danced with the flickering light and reminded me of the boats on the lake. The same way the waves keep the lights from distant boats in constant motion. I ran back inside and locked the door. I used the phone in the hall to call my dad up in Gaylord.

It took him a long time to answer; when he did, his voice made me cry.

"I'm scared," I said. "There's something weird in the sky. What should I do?" I cried like Joey, without waiting to catch my breath.

"Katie," he said. "Is that you, Katie?"

"Dad," I said. "It's horrible. There's all these lights. Just like a UFO or something. I'm alone and I'm scared."

"Different colored lights?" he asked. "Tell me what colors they are."

"Red and yellow," I said.

"Any white?"

"I guess so."

"Describe it exactly."

"I can't," I said. "I'm in the hall. There aren't any windows in here."

"Put the phone down. Go out and look at it and tell me what it looks like."

"I'm scared," I said. "What if it comes too close?"

"Go on, Katie," he told me.

My father lives up north right on the 45th parallel—halfway

between the equator and the north pole. He tells me he can walk out of his house and feel the warmth of the south and the brisk winds of the north and he knows he is home.

I put the receiver on top of the box of books I still have to go through. I went to the kitchen and looked out the window. The colors were radiant. I searched for yellow and saw the quick flashes of blues and red. A line of white light glided across the sky and then disappeared. I explained what it looked like to my father.

"I'm surprised you can see that so well," he said. "It usually doesn't shine that far south."

"What is it?" I asked.

"The northern lights," he said. "You've seen them hundreds of times up here. The aurora borealis."

When I was a child, my father used to wake me to show me the different stars in the sky. I remembered seeing something that I thought looked like fireworks.

"It's just that everything's wrong," I told him. "Joey is having nightmares and they want to leave summer camp, but I'm afraid to have them come home. I'm so afraid."

"Katie," he said. "You're afraid of something that already happened. John drowned. There's no reason to be afraid anymore."

"I can't help it," I cried. "I'm still scared."

"You should come up here," he said. "Bring the kids and you can go out in the woods. You can start looking at things again. You'll see what there is to be afraid of."

My father wanted us to live with him after John died. But his place in Gaylord is just a cabin. The furniture is sparse and there are no closets. The five rooms are connected and you can see what everyone's doing all the time. I wouldn't know where we would put all our stuff.

"I can't, Dad," I said. "I should be here."

"You're afraid of your memories, Katie," my dad said. "Get away from them. There's a lot of things in this world to be afraid of, but you can't be scared of the past. It's all over."

"We belong in this house," I said. "This is our house—John's house. I'm just trying to fix it up so we can live in it."

"Katie," he said, "listen to the cicadas." He put the phone to the window and I heard the small clicking sounds of the insects against his screen.

"Can you hear that?" he asked. "They're the seventeen-year cicadas. They're just as nasty as they were last time around."

I could hear the buzz of the cicadas and I knew my dad was watching them with his power flashlight. He would be inspecting their legs, the size of their eyes, the color of their antennas. He would capture a few—not to kill them, but to see how they acted. They would live in one of his mayonnaise jars with a hole-poked lid and in the morning, after hours of watching them, he'd set them free.

"I'm afraid this will never end, Dad," I said.

"Get away from it," he said. "Get away so you can take a look at it."

The mayonnaise jars clinked together and I knew he was anxious to start his inspection. "Come on up, Katie," he said.

The road is dark, but I keep looking for the lights of another car or a gas station on the side of the highway. I know there will be something coming up soon. This is a large interstate and I won't be alone for long. I keep my eyes forward. If I drive this speed, I can make it to camp before breakfast. I will get Marni and Joey and the three of us will navigate a shortcut to Dad's. I want Dad to show the kids his cicadas. If they want, they can catch some of their own. And soon, just as soon as I can, I will start looking too.

Lip Service Résumé

Gustav Turnquist. Norwegian—both sides of the family. His paternal grandmother, Farmor, used to complain that there was no record of her birth. It wasn't not knowing the date that bothered her—she stayed sixty-two for ten years—as much as not knowing where she had been born that made her angry. "Place," Farmor always said, "is essential to a family." She thought she might have been born in Hammerfest, the same fishing town where she grew up, but a house fire had destroyed all family records and Farmor lived her whole life with this uncertainty. Gustav was fascinated with the stories of the fire and Farmor was happy to recount the incident whenever he asked about it. For some reason which Gustav never understood, Farmor blamed the fire on the light bulbs in the family living room.

"Hammerfest was the first town in Norway to get electricity," Farmor explained to Gustav. "People had a difficult time with it."

"How can you have a hard time with light?" Gustav asked. He went over to the wall and flicked the light switch on and off. It was evening and the sun had stopped making shadows on Farmor's bare white walls.

"They used it too much," Farmor said. "Especially in the winter when it stays dark for two months. No one even knew what a fuse box was back then. They didn't know that the wiring had to be insulated."

Gustav closed his eyes and tried to imagine what it would be like to live without the sun.

"But it was summer when I stood on those rocks and watched my parents pour buckets of water on our house," Farmor said. "I remember I was barefoot and the midnight tide kept washing up cod. A whole school of lost cod. They were dead. Cold and dead up to my ankles."

"What about the ocean?" Gustav asked. It was getting dark outside and the shadows in the apartment were long, but Gustav could still see his grandmother's face across the room.

Her skin was as white and smooth as his own. "Why didn't you use the ocean?"

"We didn't have a hose to bring the water up from the shore," Farmor said. "Once the well went dry there wasn't anything anybody could do. We just stood there and watched the house burn to the ground."

Gustav knew that Farmor constantly worried about electricity. She hated lamp shades and never, ever, not even when she went down the drive to get the evening newspaper, left a light on when the house was empty.

Current Address: *3114 Holmes Avenue South, Apt. 6 D, Minneapolis, MN 55408.* Gustav kept his homosexuality a secret from Farmor as long as he could. He dreaded what she would say, what she would think of him. But after everyone else in the family knew about it, his mother started putting pressure on him to tell Farmor. He promised he would do it as soon as he felt the time was right. One afternoon in early October they were having cocktails in his small apartment. The living room looked bare; Gustav had rearranged it to make his grandmother more comfortable. The lamp shades had been removed and the couch was pushed back to the wall to hide the electrical wiring. Gustav got up to serve Farmor some more Stilton cheese and the smell was so strong, so sharp in his nostrils, that he just blurted it out.

"Farmor," he said quickly, trying not to think about it. "I'm pretty sure I'm gay."

"What does that mean?" Farmor glanced at him. She took a wheat cracker with cheese and then turned back to the magazine on her lap. Gustav subscribed to fifteen different magazines and Farmor looked at all of them when she visited.

"It means I like men," Gustav said. "I like to be with them. You know, on dates and things."

Gustav was in his fall mood. He had spent the morning packing away his summer shorts and cotton T-shirts into cardboard boxes. He hoped Farmor would hurry up and start crying or yelling or whatever she was going to do so he could get back to his house cleaning. There wasn't enough vodka in the apartment for a long fight. But like everything with Farmor, her reaction surprised him. She didn't question how he could like men as his mother and Sylvie had done, or tell him he was perverted and sick as his dad had done.

"Does that mean you won't be getting married?" Farmor asked. She closed the magazine and let her reading glasses fall forward on her chest.

"I don't think so," Gustav said. He wanted to tell her that he was having problems going out with someone for longer than a month, but she looked so dejected that he softened his response. "Maybe," he said. "Probably not for a long time."

"That's so sad," Farmor said. She picked up her glass of vodka and finished it all down at once.

Gustav thought she was talking about the end of the family line and he finished off his vodka with her.

"The best day of my life was the day I got married," Farmor told him. "I was so proud to be standing up at the altar in the Church of Norway. The most wonderful day of my life."

She reached for her purse and dumped out some papers on the couch next to the pile of finished magazines. She showed Gustav her wedding certificate so he could feel the national seal imbedded in the thin paper. Unlike her burnt birth certificate, the folded document was solid proof that in 1930 she had married an American missionary, Calvin Turnquist, who had spent a year traveling through the Scandinavian countries with a group of Episcopalian ministers.

"The Norwegians worked too long and too hard to care very much about the Church and no one wanted to talk to Calvin about salvation," Farmor explained to Gustav. "By the time he got to Hammerfest, he was sick of the strange food and the cold, slow-moving trains. The sign outside the post office told him he was in the most northerly town in the world and he didn't doubt its claim."

Farmor told Gustav that Calvin had never seen such a cold

gray sky. The dwarf birches on the side of the road were proof enough that life was just about impossible in such a climate. Good-looking strangers were an anomaly in Hammerfest and Farmor let Calvin talk about whatever he wanted. After a short courtship and a brief wedding ceremony, they left Norway and moved to a large piece of farmland three miles west of Bruce's Crossing, Iowa. Calvin quit ministering and they both started farming the land. Farmor wanted to continue working even when she started having babies, but after her fifth boy, baby-sitters became a problem—Farmor had no choice but to stay near the house and care for them herself. Her neighbors, a small group of Finns, found her strange. They didn't say anything to Farmor directly, but there was talk around Bruce's Crossing about her odd ways. They couldn't understand why she let her kids get up in the middle of the night and play in the backyard. They thought it might be characteristic of Norwegians. Calvin heard the gossip and tried to get her to change some of her habits.

"The kids are done sleeping at three o'clock," she told him. "They go to sleep after dinner. They don't want to stay in bed any longer than that."

"It's the middle of the night," he said. "Dark as can be out there."

Always cautious of electricity, Farmor had taught her children to find their way around in the dark. They were comfortable without lights, having learned when they were young that there was nothing to fear in the dark that shouldn't also be feared in the daylight.

"That's not the way things are done here in the States," Calvin tried to reason with her. "Kids get up in the daytime. Night is for sleeping." But Farmor had grown up in a land where darkness and light were never dependable and he knew he wouldn't convince her that in America night could be measured in hours, not months.

Gustav's father Jon was born in Bruce's Crossing, the youngest of eight boys. Gustav had been surprised to learn that his father had once spent eighteen years in the same place. He couldn't imagine his father growing up on a ninety-nine-acre farm in western Iowa. But Jon told Gustav that as a kid he had adored the farm.

"I worked hard alongside my brothers," Jon said.

"Why did you have to leave?" Gustav asked. "Couldn't you have stayed there? Then we wouldn't have had to move around so much."

"I started to hate the land," Jon said. "As soon as I found out that the land would never be mine, I just started to hate it."

He explained to Gustav that he couldn't see the point of working for someone else the rest of his life. He became less and less motivated to work and finally one day, furious at Farmor for having him last, confronted her about the inheritance of the property.

"Land isn't the only thing in life," Farmor told Jon. "There's a lot more world out there to worry about."

"But am I ever going to get any of this farm?" he asked. "Is any of it going to be mine?"

"This is Iowa," she said. "You know, where I grew up, we used to walk down to the cliffs and pick fish up off the rocks."

"What about the farm?" he insisted.

"We didn't need boats or fishing poles—the fish came to us," Farmor said.

"I don't care about the fish," Jon said. It was pitch black in the house. Farmor had been listening to the weather report on the portable radio and in anticipation of the coming thunderstorm had turned off all the lights.

"We made our money on that cod," she told him. "Just picked it off the rocks in bushels and sold it to the factory."

"Let's not get into it," he said. Jon could tell she was going to go on and tell him about the hours after the house fire in Hammerfest. Unlike his future son, he had no interest in hearing stories more than once. He already knew that a warm sea current, coming up from the Caribbean, blew west and ended near Hammerfest. The fish accustomed to the cold waters of the Arctic Circle swam inshore to get away from the drastic change in temperature. His mother and her family, suddenly homeless, spent the night on the beach gathering cod by the bushel. The next morning, as soon as the cod liver factory opened its doors, they sold the fish at a good price.

"Cod liver," Farmor said. "We sold all that fish and the men in Hammerfest had the best cod liver season ever. It was just chance that the current blew our way. Real good luck."

Permanent Address: *c/o Janeene Ripko Turnquist, 6571 Broadtree Court, Winona MN 55987.* Gustav was sixteen and in the dining room looking for his mother's sterling silver salt and pepper shakers when he decided that he was going to prefer men instead of women the rest of his life. He looked at himself in the mirror over the breakfront and mouthed the word "homo." His cheeks were round and puffy like the potato pancakes his mother made him for breakfast. He didn't like the look and scolded himself for putting on the extra weight. He lipped the word "fag" and the churning in the bottom of his stomach, spreading out through his chest, didn't scare him. The salt and pepper shakers were in the back of the breakfront and he removed the platters wrapped in purple felt bags and stacked them under the dining room table. He had just come from Timmo Makleva's, whose parents were bird-watching up in the Boundary Waters. Timmo had started it. He asked Gustav if he wanted to do it again and Gustav said sure. He wanted to tell Timmo it was no big deal, he had done it with at least three other guys in the junior class, but he didn't want Timmo to start doing it with anyone else, especially not Mark Ehrlich, who had just moved to Minneapolis from St. Louis. Mark was the only guy in the class with dark hair, the only one whose skin looked as if it still had a summer tan. Besides, Timmo wasn't that good. He got too nervous when it was his turn. He was always turning his head—looking at the locked bedroom door as if he expected someone to come walking in.

Gustav found the salt shaker, not the pepper, and went to the kitchen to tell his mother about his decision.

"Men?" Janeene asked, taking the salt shaker from him. "What are you going to do with men?"

"You can't ask me things like that," Gustav told her. "It's too personal."

Janeene held the pan of hollandaise sauce for Gustav to taste and offered him her advice. "I wouldn't tell your father about it," she told him. "Not just yet, anyway."

"This isn't a phase," Gustav said. "It's not like the Boy Scouts."

Gustav had been a Boy Scout for three months. He had tried karate lessons for nine weeks and glee club for fifteen days. Little League had lasted a week and he had taken one piccolo lesson.

"But that's what he'll tell you," Janeene said. She broke a carrot in half and dipped it into the pan. The sauce burned the roof of her mouth. "He'll tell you you'll get over it. Just like he's gotten over everything."

Gustav and his father had always had a rough time of it. Gustav had resented Jon ever since he found out that his mother and his father had once been married. Gustav discovered it was Jon who had moved out two weeks after Gustav was born and blamed Jon for his own restlessness, for his need to change everything in his life—his job, his friends, his lovers, even his apartments every other month. Gustav believed that if Jon had been more stable, he might have a better chance of holding down a job longer than two months at a time, a lover more than a few nights.

Professional Objective: *To obtain a position in an advertising or marketing capacity with a national firm, with an emphasis on sales or promotional strategy.* As it turned out, no one had to tell Jon about Gustav's sexual preference. He found out on his own. Jon was driving home down Hennepin around midnight one night when he saw Gustav, who was only seventeen at the time, coming out of the Saloon Bar. The car heater was broken and Jon was irritated and cold, his feet numb. Gustav was walking with a blond man and the two of them were laughing. Jon watched them disappear around the corner. The last thing he saw was the man's hand give Gustav's rear a quick pat. The traffic light changed to green and the car behind Jon's started honking. Jon drove through the intersection, watching the street corner in his rearview mirror. He went straight to Janeene's and banged on the door until she got up.

"Do you have any idea where your son is?" He stood on the front porch, his shoes in three feet of snow.

"Get in the house or go away," Janeene said. "I won't have the neighbors calling the police on me again."

Jon was too furious to argue or to ask why the police had been called before. He tracked in the snow with him. Janeene walked behind him, scooping up the large pieces of ice.

Jon went straight for the liquor stored in the shelf above the refrigerator. He searched for the J & B bottle, which was already down on the kitchen table. Janeene poured out two drinks. She shoved the pieces of snow in Jon's glass and took hers to the refrigerator for some lemon.

"I should have known he'd turn out gay," Jon said. "He grew up around too many women."

Janeene took a lemon from the vegetable drawer and sliced it in half. She squeezed it over the glasses and then sucked the insides away from the skin. She had no idea what time it was and wanted to look up at the kitchen clock, but she knew Jon would get tight-lipped about that. On the weekends Gustav had no curfew. Janeene had stopped keeping track of when he got home. She only knew that he was in bed when she got up in the morning and that he had to drink a half-gallon of Diet Coke before he could eat anything.

"Women were always telling him what to do," Jon said. "He didn't have a choice but to start imitating them."

Janeene said this was nonsense. "Look at me," she yelled at her ex-husband. "I grew up with no one around and I came out just fine with the opposite sex."

"You were the one who gave him a faggy name," Jon yelled.

"Gustav is a Viking name," Janeene said. "A good solid Viking name."

Jon tried to argue with her, but Janeene was moving too fast for his whiskey brain.

"And if you had been there when he was born, you could have named him yourself," she yelled at him.

"You always use that against me," Jon said. "I'm sick and tired of hearing the same thing over and over again."

"Not as sick as I am about it," Janeene said.

Janeene had been raised to hate men who weren't around when their babies were born. Her own father had been dancing in the streets of Oslo when she was born on the Norwegian holiday Syttende Mai. He had been all dressed up like a Viking woman—yarn braids, red lipstick, short black skirt—and drunk as a Finn when word got around that his wife had just delivered twins.

His friends pushed him into the beer wagon and pulled it to the hospital, where they dumped him on the front steps. The doctors in emergency found nothing wrong with him except a belly full of beer and they decided to let him sleep the drunk off. He spent the night on a cot in the hallway; when he got up, he stumbled to the nursery to see his wife and daughters. The nurse on duty told him to go away. She said she wouldn't let him near the ward until he came back dressed like a man. Gustav always wished he could have met his mother's father. He would have liked to have known this man—a man who would put on a dress if the occasion called for it. But he was dead long before Gustav was born—when Janeene and Sylvie were only fifteen years old. Gustav was getting drunk with his mother and Sylvie one Christmas Eve when they told him about their mother's death one hundred days after their father's death.

"She abandoned us," Janeene said. "Left us all alone in the world."

"No. She just couldn't find any reason to live without him," Sylvie said. "After he died, she stopped eating and drinking. It didn't take very long."

Sylvie turned to Gustav and said, "I don't remember that much about my father. Only that he was always on the go."

"I remember his boots," Janeene said. "His size 12 reindeer boots which he always took off right inside the kitchen door."

"When he was there," Sylvie added. "When he was there."

This information only further impressed Gustav; sometimes when he was walking home from the bus stop late at night, he would talk to this man—just to see if he could.

Jon and Janeene were still yelling and drinking when Gustav got home at 4:30 A.M. Janeene heard his key in the front door and went to bed so Gustav could tell his father what he wanted about his personal life. Jon lasted ten minutes before his head started bobbing and then he fell asleep sitting up in the chair, the drink balanced on the armrest. Gustav got the blanket from the hall closet and covered him. He pulled off Jon's shoes and socks and put them under the coffee table so his father wouldn't trip on them. Jon rolled over and knocked the blanket to the floor. Gustav covered him again. He rinsed out the glasses and stuck them in the dishwasher before going to his room. He stayed awake a long time, staring out at the starless sky, trying to remember the name of the guy he had picked up at the Saloon.

Professional Employment: *June 1980–Present, Office Manager, Macmillian Temporary Services, 6410 Cedar Lake Road, St. Louis Park, MN 55426. Supervisor—Terrence Macmillian.* Terry hired Gustav when the Cruise Lines fired him.

Gustav worked at the main office in St. Louis Park a couple days a week and, when Terry needed him, he went out in the city to work as a sub. Terry and Gustav were friends, never lovers, but lately Terry had started staying at home. "It's dangerous out there," Terry warned Gustav. "You can't trust anybody."

"This is Minneapolis," Gustav said. The phone rang and he picked it up and asked the caller to hold. "Nothing's going to happen here."

"You don't know the people you're picking up," Terry said. "You don't know where they've been."

"I'm staying away from older guys," Gustav said. "The kids at the Saloon are from the suburbs. They're doing it for the first time."

"You don't know that," Terry said. "Do you know Les Morrison went in the hospital?"

"Les Morrison lived in San Francisco," Gustav said. He cradled the phone in his shoulder and thought about getting his hair cut at lunch hour.

"He was only there one summer," Terry said. "For one summer."

"I ask where they've been," Gustav defended himself. He pushed in the blinking red light on the phone machine and spoke quickly into the receiver.

Farmor thought Gustav was crazy to do a different job every day.

"How are you ever going to know if you're good at something?" she asked him the night they were out celebrating her birthday. She had turned sixty-two again and Gustav would have preferred talking about how young she looked than to have her asking questions about his job. His shirt, just back from the cleaner's, was overstarched and he was having an uncomfortable night to begin with.

"You should stick to one thing," Farmor said. "Find one thing that you like and then keep at it. All this switching jobs isn't good for you. How are you ever going to settle down if you keep changing jobs every three months?"

"It's not my fault," Gustav argued. He broke off a piece of crust and let crumbs fall into his lap. A moment later he shook out his napkin and the crumbs scattered onto the carpeting.

The way he saw it, everyone in his family did things on the spur of the moment. The job switching wasn't his fault at all—it was hereditary. No one in the family paid attention to responsibilities; whenever his flightiness began to bother him, he got angry at his parents. He blamed them for his restlessness and Farmor, after her second piece of birthday cake, agreed with him.

"Your father's always been that way," Farmor said.

Jon and Janeene met in the lunch room at Bruce's Crossing High School in March and got married the weekend after graduation. Janeene was two months pregnant and had a difficult time standing through the backyard ceremony. The Iowa sun was hot and everything around her seemed to be spinning in slow motion. She stared at the shiny spot of saliva on the minister's chin, trying to control her dizziness. After they said their "I do"s, and the minister closed his Bible, Jon led Janeene to a lawn chair and got her a glass of ice water. Janeene picked up someone's flat purse and held it in front of her face to block the sun. The dizziness continued and she realized she would never make it through the reception. She got up and made her sister follow her into the house.

"You've got to switch places with me," Janeene told Sylvie once they were inside the cool kitchen. The room was dark, the curtains drawn to keep out the sun.

"This is your wedding day," Sylvie said. "We can't go around fooling people."

"I'm not going to make it," Janeene said. She put her head back on the refrigerator and began to cry. She was too hot to shed tears, but she whined. "I'll faint if I have to go out in that sun again."

"So what?" Sylvie asked. "Everyone'll just think it's nerves."

"They'll know I'm pregnant," Janeene cried. "Jon's mother will know. She's had eight of these. You've got to help me."

Sylvie wasn't happy. She had her eye on Jon's high school friend—the only one at the wedding who wasn't Norwegian. He had dark hair and thick bushy eyebrows. She thought he looked like Buddy Holly, whom she had just seen sing in Iowa City. Her chances with him were good; she was one of the few single girls at the wedding.

"I want to have a good time today," Sylvie said. "What am I going to do with Jon?"

"You have to do this," Janeene said. "You can have a good time the rest of your life." She reached around and undid the silk buttons that were pressing into the small of her back, then let out her breath and rubbed her damp skin. The paper tablecloths and the dry wheat grass seemed far away, somehow belonging to another day.

"Your good time got you into this situation," Sylvie said. "Looks like you should have thought of this before you planned an afternoon wedding."

Janeene closed her eyes and tried to think of Oslo. The cool water and the brisk winds and the familiar speech. They had only been in Iowa three years—sent there after their parents' deaths to live with an aunt and uncle no one in Norway had ever met. It had been hard to adjust to their life and Janeene never stopped wishing she was back in Oslo.

Sylvie continued to say no until Janeene threw a glass of water across the room. It hit the wall next to the side door and smashed to the floor, darkening the marigolds on the wall paper. Sylvie gave in. They went up to the bedroom and Sylvie changed into the white dress. She pulled her hair back in a tight bun like Janeene's and centered the daisy ring on her head. The slip scratched her legs and she pulled the garter belt up higher on her thigh. The shoes were a tight fit.

"I can't walk in them," Sylvie said. She took a few practice steps in front of the mirror. "My feet look like sausages stuffed into these ugly things."

"You can take them off as soon as you get downstairs," Janeene said. "Tell everyone you can't walk in the grass in heels. It's your day, they'll let you get away with anything."

"Except carrying a baby."

"I'm scared," Janeene said. "I'm really scared." She pulled down the shades and stretched out on her sister's bed. The pillow case smelled of Sylvie's shampoo, like the giant sunflowers lining the back forty yards of their property.

"You won't be having that thing for another seven months," Sylvie said. "Don't think about it today."

Jon was always grateful for the switch. His mother had been suspicious about the wedding date and she would know for sure something was the matter if Janeene couldn't even make it through her own wedding. Jon told Sylvie he thought both twins made beautiful brides. Sylvie stood in the receiving line, keeping her eyes on Jon's friend, who spent most of the reception dancing with a young cousin. Sylvie couldn't remember her name, but knew she wasn't a day over fifteen. Later she saw them making out behind the barn and she wanted to tear at her sister's hair. Instead she leaned over and kissed Jon right on the lips. The relatives standing on the dance floor cheered. They were drunk on homemade draft beer and stomped their feet for another. Sylvie kissed him six more times. Years later Gustav stopped speaking to Jon for seven months when he found out Jon had moved in with Sylvie two weeks after Gustav's birth. Jon justified his actions by explaining that it had all happened so fast—things just seemed to happen so fast. He told Gustav that if you looked at it the right way, he had really married both of them that day under the hot Iowa sun.

October 1979–June 1980, *Translator, Norwegian Cruise Lines, 2234 Lindale Avenue South, St. Paul MN 55116. Supervisor—Blake Bjornstein. Duties included translating advertis-*

ing copy and all public relations material. On tour duty with rotating schedule, as translator for 700 passengers. The first thing people noticed about Gustav was his hair. Blake, his direct employer and live-in lover for three months, asked him during the initial interview if his hair was real. Later, after Gustav had dumped Blake and had been fired, Blake came up to him on the dance floor at the Saloon.

"How many guys have you been with this week?" he asked.

Gustav smiled and ignored the question. He didn't think he owed Blake any explanation. He had liked the job at the Cruise Lines and he was mad at Blake for firing him. Job searching always depressed him.

"Do you even know if the guys are clean?" Blake asked. "You ever think of that?"

The bar was hot and smoky. Gustav stopped dancing and went over to his table for his drink. Blake followed him.

"You don't think it'll hit you, do you, Gustav?" Blake asked. "Just because you got a full head of blond hair, you think you can outlive everybody?"

Gustav finished his drink and then walked up to the bar for another one. A moment later Blake disappeared.

Gustav had been born blond—a full head of hair. It stayed blond until he was in his late teens and then he began to touch up the color. At first all it took was a squeeze of lemon, or a spray of Sylvie's Sun-In. But later, when the roots turned dark brown, he started getting it done professionally.

The minute Farmor saw him, she forgave Janeene for having the baby seven months after the wedding night. She forgave Jon for taking a job in Minneapolis, but she refused to forgive Sylvie for carrying on with Jon while Janeene was in the hospital.

Jon was in the Naked Reindeer rubbing Sylvie's feet when Gustav made his first appearance into the world. He had been a father for four hours before he finally called home. The day had started out innocently enough—Jon wanted to take Sylvie on a tour of Minneapolis. Farmor said he should get out of the apartment, because the way he was carrying on with Sylvie was getting on everyone's nerves.

"They're identical—twins," Farmor said to him. "How much of a difference can there be?"

Jon wanted to tell Farmor about the wedding, but he saw Janeene standing at the kitchen window nine months pregnant and he couldn't think of what to tell her.

The night before a snowstorm had dropped fifteen inches of soft powder on the city and the streets were empty. Jon drove slowly down to the warehouse district on the other side of the river and parked the car outside the Pillsbury Dough Company. It was Saturday and Sylvie was unimpressed with the large gray factory. She tried, but she couldn't smell any bread baking. Jon leaned over and kissed her, unaware that his wife had gone into labor. Half an hour later Sylvie pulled away and told him she wanted to get drunk before they made love.

"I wouldn't know how to do it otherwise," she said. "I've been drunk every other time I went all the way."

Jon drove down to Snoose Alley where the Norwegian let him buy liquor even though he wasn't nineteen. Janeene had been pregnant for so long that Jon had forgotten how much women liked to drink—something which Gustav would never forget. They finished off a pint of vodka and made love on an empty street near Lake of the Isles. Right when they finished, a city truck drove by and sprayed salt on the windshield. Sylvie pulled the rearview mirror to one side so she could touch up her lipstick and told Jon she was starving. Jon redid his belt and told her about the fish fry at the Naked Reindeer.

"It's ocean perch," he said. "All you can eat for two dollars."

"I could eat a whole room full of fish," Sylvie said. "Even if it does come down a lousy river."

Jon drank and watched Sylvie finish off three helpings of fish. He reached under the table and pulled off her boot. He began rubbing her feet, and when she wiped the tartar sauce

from her mouth with the large paper napkin, he told her that
he loved her.

Education: *Bachelor of Arts in Scandinavian Studies, 1977,
St. Olaf College, St. Paul, MN.* Farmor, Janeene, and Sylvie took him to Trondheim for St. Olav's day so they could
celebrate Gustav's graduation from the college with the same
name, different spelling. Gustav had heard that there was a
huge gay population in Trondheim and he thought it was time
he did it with a true Norwegian. Gustav left the three of them
drinking coffee and eating lutefisk and took a bus to the other
side of town. A guy from the Saloon had written the address
on a napkin and Gustav found the nightclub without any problems. Inside, the music, the drinks, even the people were familiar to him and it didn't take long to find someone who
would take him home. His apartment was full of light—even
so far south, Gustav thought he could see traces of the midnight sun. The guy was drunk and Gustav liked the strange Norwegian sounds he made. He left while the guy was sleeping
and walked back to the hotel through the crowded streets of
the city.

Janeene and Sylvie were still sitting up at the cafe with a liter
of red wine between them. Farmor had gone to bed early,
excited about the train trip to Hammerfest the next day.

Gustav sat down with them and ordered some vodka.

"A man?" Sylvie leaned over and sniffed his neck.

Gustav laughed and pushed her away. "Just a kid," he said.

"It's probably just as well to stay away from men," Janeene
said. "Stick to kids."

"Money," Sylvie said. "If a man's got money—he's okay in
my book."

"Then why'd you live with Jon so long?" Janeene laughed.

Gustav looked at them and thought they both looked too
young to have a son his age.

"Never left. He just never left," Sylvie said. She was drunk and wanted to laugh. "It's great to have holidays just because some corpse grew some hair."

Janeene let out a hoot and Gustav asked them to explain.

"It's true," Janeene said. "Farmor just told us. The reason they made King Olav a saint was because they dug him up after he'd been in the ground for a while and they found that his hair and his nails were still growing."

Gustav started to tell them about the battle in 1030, but it didn't fit the holiday mood.

"He was gay," Gustav said. "Old King Olav was gay."

Janeene slammed down her wine glass and brushed the hair out of her face. "All those Vikings liked each other."

"I'd be one too," Sylvie said. "You've got the right idea, Gustav." She put her arm around Gustav's shoulder and they toasted to one another.

"I feel like this could last forever," Gustav said. "It just feels like it's going to last forever."

"You're Norwegian," Sylvie said. She leaned over and rubbed her long fingernails against his cheek. "You'll stay young for a long time."

"But not forever," Janeene told him.

Gustav hadn't been talking about his youth as much as he had been talking about the ease, the freedom of his life. He had luck—Norway, Minneapolis, St. Paul, everywhere he went. He saw it continuing the rest of his life, whether or not he had to get old. It was such a surprise when he found out it couldn't last. Gustav was more surprised than anybody.

Personal: *Single. Enjoy tennis and water skiing and fishing.* Once the unemployment checks stopped, Gustav got desperate and started going through both the morning and evening newspaper as soon as it was delivered to the grocery store down the corner from his house. He mailed his résumé to Bosman Airlines the day the ad ran in the *Minneapolis Star.* A week later Ms. Bosman, the company president, called him and asked him out to dinner.

"We can meet at Les Figurines," Ms. Bosman said. "How about nine o'clock? Have a drink at the bar so I won't feel guilty if I'm a few minutes late."

Gustav untangled the cord and pulled the phone over to the calendar above the sink.

"Tonight's Friday," he told Ms. Bosman.

"I know it's a date night," she said. "But could you cancel those plans? I really need to fill this flight attendant spot. It's the holidays and everyone and their uncle wants to fly to Las Vegas."

He didn't tell her that the Saloon had closed for good in January and that the last time he went out he had gone to a movie and was back home in his apartment alone by eleven-thirty.

Ms. Bosman was more than a few minutes late. Gustav had already had two vodkas. The young bartender had passed him a matchbook with his phone number on the inside front cover. Gustav glanced at it quickly before tossing it under the bar stool. He followed Ms. Bosman into the dining room and she ordered a bottle of red wine from the busboy who brought them hand towels.

"I've got your résumé here," she said after the steward opened the wine. "It's pretty cut and dry. Why don't you expand it a little? Tell me more about yourself."

Gustav, already buzzed from the vodka, raised his glass and began telling Ms. Bosman about himself. He told her about Norway, about the Laplanders fishing by his grandmother's homesite. Ms. Bosman listened attentively, even while ordering the meal, and he kept talking about his family. In between courses, she would dip her pinky into a large tube of lip gloss and paint a thick streak across her lips. It was an awkward gesture and she spent another five minutes smoothing it over, trying to get the globs out of the corners of her mouth. Somehow it stained her teeth; when she smiled, the pink shimmering splotches smiled too. During the meal the gloss got on everything: the edge of the water glass, the linen napkin, even on her collar when she turned her head to look at the dancers in the center of the room. Gustav thought she had awfully thin lips and he wasn't surprised when he saw that the waiter's jacket was stained with the pink stuff.

Ms. Bosman handed him his résumé. "It seems that you've only worked for men," she said. "Tell me what you think of women."

Ms. Bosman was flirting with him. He could tell by the way she was staring at him, by the way she kept redoing her lips, by the way she had let him go on and on.

Gustav poured the last of the wine from the bottle without offering it to Ms. Bosman first. She would want him to have it anyway. He knew that if Farmor were there she would recite an old Norwegian superstition—whoever finished the bottle of wine got married before the year's end. If Janeene were at the table, she would tell him that he should lie and tell Ms. Bosman that he had worked with plenty of women at his other jobs. And Sylvie would tell him that he should tell Ms. Bosman to try a thin paintbrush instead of her fingers. Gustav drank his wine and smiled at Ms. Bosman.

"Women? I love women. I've always loved women," he said truthfully.

Ms. Bosman tilted her head slightly to one side so that the candlelight caught her face at an attractive angle. Gustav, comfortable in the near darkness, brought his napkin up to her mouth and wiped the lipstick from her teeth before he kissed her.

References upon request. He was still his father's son. Like the cod that blew off course into the Arctic Circle. He could try the change.

The Long White

Only two things have ever happened in my hometown—Good Hart, Michigan. The first was in 1967 when Jurff Pancy shot his wife and St. Bernard and left them to rot in the house. Their house is set back from M119 and it took the police three months to find out they were dead. Good Hart is in northern Michigan, thirty miles south of the Mackinac Bridge, and people never let on that they care about other people's business. Lola Matela runs the General Store in Cross Village and she kept pestering everyone who came in about whether they had seen Enid Pancy. She knew that Jurff was working road construction and that, whenever he was out of town, Enid went up to the General for fresh eggs and milk and an hour's worth of gossip. As the weeks passed, Lola got worried and finally called the State Police. They drove out to the house to see if there was a problem. That's when they found them—Enid all shot up on her living room floor with the dog dead beside her. The cold spring had kept some of the decay from setting in, but the police said the stench and the maggots were everywhere. They went after Jurff—brought him downstate and locked him up. That August they let him go. He said he didn't kill Enid or the dog and no one could prove that he did.

People just knew he was the one. He looks like the kind of person who could have done something like that. His eyebrows go straight across his forehead—it looks like he just has one. Everyone in town believes the house is still jinxed and the police want to burn it to the ground. Jurff moved up to Indiantown. He still comes into Good Hart once in a while. People stare at him, some of the men mumble good morning his way, but no one talks to him directly.

The second thing that happened in Good Hart was on account of the first. It was just this past week, when my brother Robin Conaway, lead singer for the Kingbees, the best rockabilly band in the world, played his guitar in front of Gert's Gas Stop for sixteen hours straight. He stood right off M119 for all the tourists and townies to hear and played without stopping except to use the bathroom and a couple of times to eat something. Everyone from Good Hart showed up and most of the folks from Bliss, Levertown, and Cross Village came down to see what was going on. They sat on the hoods of their cars with picnic lunches and drank beer and pop. Gert sold everything edible she had stocked in the Gas Stop. I got Robin some Life Savers and gave them to him when his throat was dry. The day was full of sunshine and it seemed like a holiday or the state fair. Robin wore his black jeans and a white T-shirt with stick-on letters that read "To sing the blues you gotta live them." At dusk he put on his leather jacket and zipped it under his chin. With his hair greased back and that wide collar around his neck, he looked like a wild bird. When he turned his face up to the sky, it seemed as if he were miles away from us. The night got cold and I sat right near him, wrapped in an itchy army blanket, with my back against the gas pump. He dedicated his last song, "Islands Beyond," to Mom and after he finished playing he couldn't even whisper, his voice was so worn out. Some people clapped and Mom cried.

Robin didn't want to play in Good Hart. Mom made him do it.

She wanted Robin to play because she said it was time to change Good Hart's reputation. She said she was sick and tired of people only talking about Good Hart as the place where a man shot his wife and dog and walked away a free man. The murders happened twenty years ago, five years before I was born, and Mom thinks that people should be talking about something else. Mom cares a lot about what other people say. She works up at Fort Michilimackinac right by the bridge and she sees plenty of folks from out of town. Whenever she tells them she lives in Good Hart, they lean over the counter and start whispering things. Their eyes get all excited and they want to know if she's friends with the guy who shot his wife. They want to know if he goes to church, where he works, and if he plays cards with the people from town. They want to know his address, what he buys at the General Store, if he carries a gun. Mom said when people say Good Hart, they think murder. She said you have to make folks forget—especially in Good Hart, where nothing much happens. That's why last October she started getting after Robin to do something about it. He didn't have a choice—she never would have stopped going after him.

"You can do it with your music," Mom told him. "You can change things with your music."

"How's that?" Robin asked.

"I want you to get the band to play here," she said. Mom was in the kitchen jarring pickles. The vinegar got into the knife cuts around her fingernails and she was irritated long before Robin came by. I had been trying to help her, but when she gets annoyed, there's no way to please her. She told me to start unmaking the beds. She wanted the sheets, blankets, and even mattress pads washed. It's a hard job to do alone, but I was happy to get out of her way.

Robin had been avoiding coming around the house, because Mom wouldn't talk about anything else. If he tried to change the subject, she'd steer it back to him doing something for Good Hart.

"We do play around here, Ma," Robin said. "We just finished three nights in Pelston at the Crooked Lake Club."

"Pelston doesn't suffer like Good Hart does," Mom said. "They don't have the problems we have."

"Ma," Robin said. "The band sings wherever you want us to. We sang at Kris Taklo's wedding in Cross Village because you asked me to. All those Finns. No one spoke a word of English and we didn't know what kind of songs to play, but we did it.

We sang at Levertown's centennial and at Mackinac's twenty-fifth birthday party."

"It's not the same thing," Mom said. She picked off a pinch from the clump of fresh dill on the counter and sprinkled it in the bottom of each jar. I had picked the dill from the paths near the railroad tracks the day before. It's easy to find in the sunshine. The green leaves stick out against the burned crabgrass, which in late autumn is a dry yellow color.

"What do you want me to do?" Robin started to light a cigarette and then blew out the match. Dad was just two nights home and Robin never smokes in front of him, not that Dad would care. But Robin says that years ago when Dad was better he used to tell Robin there was something unnatural about a person blowing smoke from his mouth and nostrils.

I piled the sheets and mattress pads into the center of Mom's bedroom and wrapped them into a ball. I tied the end corners into knots and tried to lift it. It was too heavy to carry down to the washer. I didn't want to interrupt Robin and Mom so I rolled the bundle to the back door and kicked it down the basement steps. The steps are planks of old rotting wood and the bundle got stuck halfway. I gave it another kick and sent it to the bottom. They were still arguing in the kitchen. Mom had her back to the sink holding a fistful of yellow cucumbers and Robin was at the table, flipping through the labels I had printed for the pickle jars. He had just started dyeing his hair black and it always took me by surprise to see him with his blond curls gone. The guys in the band thought they should all look alike, so Robin's girlfriend Aleo washed everyone's hair with the same pack of Clairol Instant Color. His eyebrows are still blond, but when he plays he wears dark sunglasses.

"I want you to play here in Good Hart," Mom told him.

"Where?" He stood up and went over to her. He took the cucumbers out of her hands and started moving around the floor with her. Robin can usually get Mom out of her foul moods by making her dance. But that day she wouldn't have any of his fooling around. I don't think he knew how serious she was. "There's no place to play music here in Good Hart," Robin said.

"Play at Gert's," Mom said. She pushed Robin's hands away and went back to slicing cucumbers.

"At Gert's?" Robin asked. "Where would we play there? Next to the cans of motor oil?"

"You can play outside," Mom said. The knife hit the cutting board in sharp raps and Robin sat back down. He tilted the chair against the wall and put his feet on the kitchen table.

"Outside?" Robin said. "Are you crazy? The band's not going to play outside. It's October."

I sneaked out back to sit with Dad. He always stayed away from family arguments. He was gone so much of the time that he couldn't keep up with what was going on and let Mom take care of things. His job on the iron ore ships kept him away from Good Hart from May to late September. The ships ride the Great Lakes from Toledo up all the way across Superior to Duluth. If the weather was warm and the lakes didn't freeze, he would stay on until November, but the Upper Peninsula was hit with snow the first of October and Dad got sent home. Even when he wasn't working, he couldn't get the lakes out of his mind. In nice weather he sat out back staring at Lake Michigan, and when it got cold he'd sit inside, staring out. Robin said he used to talk more, but I don't remember him ever saying much.

The night's shadows crawled up the hill from shore. I stood beside Dad and listened to Mom and Robin arguing.

"Do you want to watch television with me?" I asked. The air was cold and I pulled the sides of his jacket together and did the button over his stomach. His eyes were open, but his stare across the lake was blank and I turned to see what he was looking at. Lake Michigan at Good Hart is an open bay and the waves come in as strong as the ocean. The tides beat against the sands with such force that dunes have formed along the coastline down to the bluffs.

Dad shook his head.

"There are some different programs on tonight," I said. "It's the new season. You can't say you're sick of them, because you've never seen them before."

"Makes me lonely," Dad said.

"Lonely," I repeated. "Television's not supposed to make you lonely. It's supposed to make you unlonely. It's like having company around all the time."

"Lonely," he said. He fell silent again and I watched the lake with him until the goose bumps on my legs began to ache.

"Come on in, Dad," I said. "It's getting cold."

He kept staring at the water. His face was thick with wrinkles and he always looked tired. Mom said the Great Lakes were beating him. The year before he stayed on ship until December and when he got home his face was deep red as if he had just been out in a snowstorm. He told me it was Lake Superior's Demon who reached up and kissed his face. She wouldn't let go and he was held in her arms for hours. The red would never fade, not until he went back to her. I wanted to know what the Demon looked like—if she was a mermaid or a witch, and Dad told me she was neither.

"She's beautiful," Dad told me one night last winter. "But difficult to understand."

"What does that mean?" I insisted.

"She's a mysterious woman who hides in the waves and plays games with the iron ore ships even in the winter when the ice and wind keep everything else quiet."

Dad spoke real soft and I got up from the couch and sat down near him to hear what he was saying. He put his hands on my shoulders and I swear I could almost feel the cold from Superior. "She's possessive all right. She keeps her victims for herself. I've never seen her give one up. Not after she's claimed them for her own."

He told me that if he was ever lost in Superior not to go looking for him. "I'll be at the bottom," he said. "With the Demon."

I took off my sweater and wrapped it around Dad's neck. The arms were too short to tie together so I tucked them into his collar.

"They'll stop fighting if you tell them to," I said. "Why don't you come in and tell them to quit fighting?"

"Listen to her," he said. "There's no man who can beat the woman in your mother."

Some of the things he said didn't make sense, and I laughed.

"I'm going to tell her you said she looked like a man," I teased.

"Not a man," he said. "A tree. She's like a tree." Dad finished his bottle of Budweiser and let it drop to the ground. I went to the shed where he keeps a case stacked and opened another. Dad always drank quietly. Never enough that you could tell something was wrong, but he drank all the time when he was home. The shed reminded me of late summer. Garbage bags full of dried grass were still stacked in the corner and I blew the old smell from my nostrils.

Dad took the bottle without a word. I left him and went back inside. Robin and Mom were still fighting. They hadn't turned on any lights and they fought in the dark kitchen. I put on the television, but kept the sound off.

"We play for money, Ma," Robin said. "We're good. People pay us great money to play in their bars. We don't have to play in someone's parking lot."

"I'm asking you to do it," Mom said. "That's all. I think it's important for you to play there and I want you to."

"Why?" Robin said. "What's going to happen to Good Hart if the Kingbees play at Gert's?"

"Plenty," Mom said. "People from around here can start forgetting about those horrible murders."

"They won't forget," Robin argued. "They'll just have more to talk about."

"You don't understand people," Mom said. "You don't know how their minds work like I do."

"This is ridiculous," Robin said. "Even if I wanted to, I couldn't get the guys to agree. We made a pact more than a year ago to only play when there's money. How can I tell them that we have to sing in front of a highway for nothing?"

"What about Aleo?" Mom asked. She lowered her voice and said something I couldn't hear. I got up from the couch and walked softly across the room toward the kitchen, staying close to the wall to keep from sight.

"What are you talking about?" Robin was standing by the door with one hand on the glass as if he was ready to walk out. He turned around. "What does Aleo have to do with this?"

Robin thinks Mom doesn't like Aleo because she's Indian, but that isn't true. Mom doesn't like her because Aleo and Robin live together in an apartment down near Bliss and they've never had Mom to visit. "If they're going to live together, they should at least have me over for coffee," Mom complains to me. "They don't have to have the whole family. I understand they don't want to have Dad. He'd just sit there looking for water. But I should be invited. It doesn't have to be a fancy dinner. Just coffee. I could even bring a housewarming gift. I could bring the coffee. But never to be invited? I've never heard of such a thing."

I've been to the apartment a couple of times and Robin's right—it is no big deal. Just two rooms with four walls each. It's not very clean and the band keeps their instruments there when they don't have a gig, so there isn't any place to sit anyway.

Mom said something I didn't catch, but whatever it was made Robin mad. He just about exploded.

"Are you saying because she's Indian that she should care

about some murders that happened twenty years ago?" Robin yelled at Mom. "Is that what you mean?"

"Jurff Pancy was one of her people." Mom forgot about keeping quiet and started yelling at Robin.

"What's that supposed to mean?"

"I would think she'd want to do something about the murders so people could forget them. That's all I'm saying."

"She doesn't care what people say," Robin shouted. "What do you think? Because she's Indian she should feel guilty? Like she was responsible for those murders?"

"She might have some pride and want to clean up her heritage," Mom said. "You know what people talk about around here. You know how people treat the Indians."

"And you think it's because Jurff Pancy was a nut and shot his wife?" Robin was furious. "Every time some Finn gets drunk and does something crazy, I don't see you doing anything about it. Do you watch out for every damn Finn in Good Hart?"

"If they'd murdered their wives I would." Mom was yelling at the top of her lungs. She picked up one of the pickle jars and smashed it to the floor. Robin walked out of the house.

Mom pushed open the door and screamed into the night. "I bet you Aleo spends time with that maniac out in Indiantown."

Robin backed his truck down the driveway. The high beams shone through the kitchen window, outlining Mom. The tires spun the gravel and screeched onto the blacktop highway. At that moment, with the light hitting her, Mom did look like a tree. From the shoulders down, her body was all the same shape. Like the base of the oaks on our property, she is sturdy. Her waist is as thick as her shoulders. She stood with her arms folded under her chest, waiting for Robin to come back and tell her he would do anything she wanted.

I got the dustpan and broom out of the pantry and began sweeping up the broken glass.

"Don't move," I said. Mom was barefoot and the pickle juice

ran in trails around her toes. The jar shattered into pieces so small I couldn't see them, but when I put my hand to the floor, the sharp shards stung my skin. Mom ignored me and walked across the kitchen and outside to yell at Dad. I cleaned up the mess and dumped it into the incinerator. The tiles were still sticky and I poured dishwashing soap on them and wiped it around with a sponge. The suds were too hard to get up with the wet sponge so I laid down paper toweling.

Mom came back inside. "Don't waste all that toweling, Carenne." She knelt beside me and in one sweep scooped up the paper towels lined on the floor. "Robin doesn't understand how important this is to me," she said.

"I don't think the guys would agree to it," I told her. "They like to play for money now."

"I'm not asking for their whole lives," Mom said. "I'm asking them to play one time. That's all."

The television cast a violet hue across the living room. The figures moved back and forth on the screen, changing the patterns of light on the furniture. I took my knapsack from the corner and went to my bedroom to do homework without saying good night to Mom or Dad. Mom was busy with her own thoughts and Dad was still out back staring at the water. I lay on my bed and tried to read some social studies, but the smell of the vinegar from the pickle juice trapped under my fingernails made me queasy and I couldn't concentrate. A while later I heard the door slam and I went to the window. Mom was leading Dad into the house. He had both hands on her shoulders and they walked in baby steps to the back door. It always took Dad time to get his land legs back. It was the same way when he first got on ship. Robin and I saw him off one year when the ship was anchored in Sault Ste. Marie. When the ship passed through the Soo Locks into Lake Superior we could see Dad walking on the deck holding onto the guy in front of him, both hands balanced on his shoulders, hardly moving at all.

II

The next week Robin left on the Kingbee tour without talking to Mom. He came by once, but she gave him the silent treatment. Not a word. She acted like she didn't hear a thing when he tried to talk to her.

The day he left, he came by school and gave me a lift. I had been waiting for the bus in the wind and when I got in the van I put my face against the heater to get rid of the stinging in my cheek. I could feel the skin burn and Robin told me to be careful.

"You want to drive up to the bridge?" Robin asked. We parked in front of his apartment. The front door was wide open and I saw Dooley, the bass player, moving out some of the sound equipment. "Aleo can take you home."

"She's not going with you?" I knew the band was planning a long tour—they were going to make it to California, but Aleo always traveled with them.

"Not this time," he said. "She doesn't want to be away that long."

This was news to me. "How long you going to be gone?" I asked. The truck started to roll back down the incline and Robin reached down for the hand brake.

"We'll be back in late spring." He went around and opened the door for me. He held out his hand for my knapsack so I could jump down.

"You'll miss Dad," I said. "He says he's leaving in April this year."

"I don't think he'll notice," Robin said. "I told him good-bye."

"I'm sorry Mom won't talk to you."

"She's a stubborn one," Robin said. "Once she gets going on something she won't stop."

The guys were in a good mood. They smiled and told me if I was ready to quit school I could travel as the band's mascot. Dooley asked Robin for a hand and they carried the keyboard out to the van. Aleo was in the corner and she ruffled my hair when I went up to her.

"You make me think of the old Robin," she said. "Before he decided to dye his hair dark." The ends of my hair were knotted from the day at school and Aleo brushed them out with her long nails. Aleo is sometimes distant with me, but that day she was being friendly enough.

"It's not so great being blonde," I told her. "Everyone knows you're a Finn. They call you stubborn without even knowing you."

Aleo laughed hard. She threw back her head and smacked it against the wall.

"Are you all right?" I asked.

Aleo rubbed the spot where she had hit the wall, but didn't stop laughing. She has large white teeth and her skin is always shiny. Right below her ear, along her jaw line, she has a birthmark that looks like someone halfway outlined her face with a dark pencil. She told me all the girls in her family have the almost identical mark.

"Why aren't you going with the Bees?" I asked her.

"I don't like California," she said. "Too many people there."

"I've never been," I said. The wind blew in the open door and I moved away from the draft.

"Neither have I," she said. "But I know I wouldn't like it. I don't even like Green Bay."

She went to the counter which splits the two rooms and asked if I wanted a drink.

"A Coke, please," I said.

"No. It has to be something stronger," she said. "Your brother is leaving on tour. A transcontinental tour. We have to have something big to toast to the Kingbees going away."

Dooley was sitting on the bed stringing one of the guitars. "I'll take one of what you're fixing," he said.

"No way," Aleo said. "The band's having beer. The drinks are for those of us who are staying."

She poured something clear into a large plastic cup and told me to take it for a roadie. It smelled like pine cones, but the cup was dirty and small dark flakes floated around the top. I got in the van with the guys and Robin and Aleo followed in his truck. The Kingbees kept kidding me about joining up with them and we joked around about life in California. I gave Dooley my drink. He asked me if I wanted a beer instead. He pointed to the cooler, but I told him I had homework to do. They didn't say anything about playing in Good Hart and I wondered if Robin had even told them about Mom's idea.

We pulled into the rest area near Fort Michilimackinac. The fort is closed most of the winter and some people stop to take photographs of the Mackinac Bridge. The bridge joins Lake Huron and Lake Michigan and people say that is where Huron, dirty from Detroit, pollutes Lake Michigan. But that day both lakes were rough and the waves jumped over the break wall like it was nothing. The water was the same gray as the suspension wires outlining the bridge. Robin and Aleo were behind us, but the guys sat facing forward. When I went to slide the door open, Dooley shook his head.

"Give them another minute," he said. "Your homework can wait."

I sat back on my knapsack feeling stupid and stared out the window at the cars passing over the bridge. A few minutes later Robin came and told me Aleo was waiting in the truck. A light snow had started to fall. The flakes danced down quickly from the low clouds. White lines were beginning to form at the base of the trees and street lamps.

"You tell Mom I said good-bye." Robin gave me a hug. His leather jacket smelled new. "Take care of yourself."

"Okay," I said. I swung my knapsack over my shoulder and climbed into the truck. Aleo backed up and let the van go in front of her before turning around to head south on M119. I looked through the back window and she kept watch in the rearview mirror as the van disappeared over the slope of the bridge. We started for home. The fields on both sides

of the two-lane road were dull with acres of cut grass, the
fences beaten down from the wind. The low clouds lifted, but
evening crept across the lake and covered the fresh light with
dusk. Aleo made a left turn down a dirt road which was lined
with pine trees and soon we lost most of the remaining light.
She slowed down and drove over a wood bridge that covered
a dry ditch. On the other side was a row of shedlike buildings.
We pulled up in front of one and Aleo stopped the truck. The
windows were covered with sheets, but in the bottom corner
of one a red neon sign flashed the word BEER.

"Come on in," she said. "I need a pack of cigarettes. You
want something to drink?"

"I'm only fifteen," I said. "I can't go in there."

"Sure you can," she said. "We're in Indiantown. If you can
stand up, you can be in the bar."

"This is Indiantown?" I asked.

"Would your mom kill me if she knew I took you here?" She
reached for her jacket and pulled it over her shoulders, like a
cape, without zipping it.

"I won't tell her," I promised.

I got out of the truck to get a look at the place. The only
movement came from the flashing of the small sign in the
window.

"Is this it?" I asked.

"What did you think it would look like?"

"Not like this," I told her. No one from Good Hart goes to
Indiantown. People are always talking about the fights and the
drinking and the fires and the incest that go on in Indiantown.
I was disappointed by the overpowering silence, the low building the same gray color as an owl's wing, and the flashing neon
sign that I thought should say more than just BEER. I wanted
something besides Aleo's word that this was really Indiantown.

"How do people know it's Indiantown?" I asked.

Aleo shrugged and walked toward the bar without waiting
for me. The building next door was boarded from inside with
planks of wood painted blue and the side yard was filled with

rolls of barbed-wire fencing. I hurried to follow Aleo. We made tracks in the new snow.

The bar looked like the recreation room over at the high school. The tables in the room were long, with legs that could be folded under. Chairs were stacked along the paneled walls. There was no jukebox or bar or even liquor bottles, like the places where the Kingbees sing. Robin sneaks me into those places, but makes me sit on the stage. I can't move around. I have to ask permission even if it's just to go to the bathroom. Aleo pointed to a table off to one side and told me to go over there. I kept my coat on. She went up to the two old men drinking in the other corner and said hello. I tried not to stare. The sign taped to the wall next to me said something about Thursday night. That's all I could read of the faint pencil marks on the tattered piece of paper.

Aleo put two plastic cups of beer and a pack of cigarettes on the table in front of me.

"You flushed?" she asked. She touched my cheeks, which I figured were probably red from holding them up to the truck heater. Her own skin was smooth and she never wore makeup.

"I'm okay," I said. I rubbed my cheek to get the red out.

"Do you drink?" She pointed to the beer on the table.

"Sometimes," I said. "At dances and things."

"That's probably when I started too." She lit a cigarette and the bar fell into silence. The men weren't talking, just sitting there drinking and watching us.

"How's your dad?" Aleo ground out the half-smoked cigarette. The glowing embers broke into tiny pieces. I blew on them and they sparked back in my face.

"The same," I said. I took a sip of the beer and tasted foam. It always surprised me. It tastes just like the foam on top of a soda, but it's not sweet. I sipped some more.

"Not getting any better?" she asked.

"Not getting any worse," I lied.

"Your mom okay?" she asked.

"She's not talking to Robin," I said. "Did you know that?"

Aleo ignored my question and drank her beer. Three young guys walked in and stood for a moment brushing the snow from their jackets. Aleo knew them and went over to say hello. She didn't tell me to follow so I stayed put. I counted the number of times the red sign flashed on and off. I lost count once and started again. I finished my beer and bit the plastic cup into strips. Aleo came back with another cup of beer and told me she was going to play pool. I stuffed the plastic pieces into my coat pocket.

"You okay here?" she asked.

I shrugged.

"When you go home you can tell everyone you partied in Indiantown," she said. "That'll give them a shock. Won't it?"

"It sure will," I said.

The bar was getting warm—the space heater in the corner was red as the glowing embers of her cigarette. Aleo pulled her sweater over her head and threw it on top of her coat. She wore a green long underwear T-shirt with buttons down to her jeans.

The beer made a knot in my stomach, but it tasted nice and salty like roasted peanuts so I drank it. No one was looking at me, so I took off my coat and walked over to the pool table. I half sat on the window ledge and watched them play. They weren't talking much, but I could tell Aleo was having a good time. She started drinking bottled beer and gave me the bottle when it was her turn to shoot. I had three lined up on the window sill. Aleo laughed when she saw them.

"You better hurry and drink up," she said. "We're supposed to be splitting those things." It felt strange to hold the dark bottle in my hand. The neck is longer and thinner than a Coke bottle and I was still having a problem with the taste. I held the bottle of beer just like Dad and wondered what would happen if I let it drop to the floor. My eyes were heavy and I felt like I could fall asleep, but then Aleo came over and told me it was time she took me home.

The guys quit playing pool and one of them walked us to the door. I waited half inside, half outside while he kissed Aleo good-bye. The snow was falling heavily. It had formed a short barricade around the bar and I kicked the soft piles with the tops of my tennis shoes. Aleo had her hands in her coat pocket, but her face was smashed into the guy's. I walked out to the truck, I pulled the sleeve of my coat over my hand and brushed the snow from the windshield. She came out a few minutes later and started the engine. When I got in the truck, the heater was blasting cold air.

I could taste the beer in my mouth, but it felt like it was everywhere—in my ears, the back of my throat, floating around in my stomach. It was even in my nostrils. I held my breath so I wouldn't get sick, but then I remembered something I had thought of while Aleo was playing pool.

"Hey," I said. "Does Jurff Pancy ever go in that bar?" The windshield wipers beat back and forth, carving out triangular shapes on the glass.

"Jurff Pancy's a free man," Aleo said. "He should be able to do what he wants without everyone getting into his business."

"I'd be afraid if he was ever in a place where I was," I told her. "He scares me half to death."

"Why's that?" Aleo asked. The smoke from her cigarette danced up my nose and I coughed into my hand. The road curved as we followed the lake. We drove through Cross Village. The General Store was dark except for the single porch light and I knew it must be after ten.

"He has funny eyes. Evil eyes," I said. "I think he wants to kill again."

Aleo opened the window and tossed out her cigarette. "Jurff Pancy was judged an innocent man," she said. "I don't remember anyone finding any evidence that he shot his wife."

"His dog too," I reminded her.

"No one has any right to say he's guilty."

"But he did it," I said. "Everyone knows that."

"You tell me how," Aleo said.

"Who else would have done it?" I asked.

"And that's how you tell if someone's murdered someone else? Because there's no one else to blame it on?"

I didn't like the way my stomach was skipping around when we took the curves. My tongue was thicker than usual and I was having problems swallowing.

"You're just like your mom," Aleo snapped at me. "You repeat things without thinking what they mean."

"We're not the only ones who say them," I said. I was confused at the way the conversation was going.

"And why isn't she talking to Robin?" Aleo said. "There's no reason he should play in Good Hart. That's not going to change anything."

"She just wants him to get the Kingbees to play once," I said.

"Does she think that will get people to forget about some gossip that's been around for twenty years?" Aleo said. "The Finns are still going to blame the Indians. Who does your mom think she is anyway? It won't change a thing. People will just think he's as crazy as your father for playing music at a gas station."

"Dad's not crazy," I said. I put my head against the window and the cold glass made me stop sweating a little.

"I'm not blaming him," Aleo said. "He's had a tough life." A car passed on the other side of the road and its headlights shone through the truck. Aleo's face turned deep blue before disappearing into the darkness again.

"Dad's not crazy," I said.

"Well, you have to admit, he's a little different," she said.

"Why'd you kiss that guy good-bye?" I asked.

"What?"

"Does Robin know you kiss guys good-bye?" My tongue was halfway down my throat and wasn't helping at all when I tried to talk, but I had to make her quit saying those mean things about Dad.

"What are you talking about?" Aleo asked.

"You kissed him on the lips," I shouted. "Does Robin know you make out with guys when he's gone?"

"Shh," Aleo said. "Don't scream like that."

The inside of the cab was suffocating me. I was furious that she was trying to kill me with her cigarette smoke, making it so I couldn't breathe. When she slowed to take the figure eight before our property, I reached for the door handle and threw myself out of the truck.

I don't remember falling—only landing. I hit the ice on the road face first. The force knocked some teeth out. I could feel blood mixing with the beer in my stomach and I threw up. The raw skin on my knees rubbed against my jeans when I tried to sit up to get off the road. I was afraid of a car coming around the curve and running over me, but the pain was too much to stand. I dragged myself to the edge of the road. When I got to the soft snow, I put my face against the coolness and started to cry.

Aleo pulled the truck around and turned the bright lights on me.

"What the hell?" she yelled. She came running at me. "What are you doing?"

She put her hands on my shoulders and forced me to sit up.

"Are you all right?" she asked. "Did you hurt yourself?"

"I hate you," I said. I tried to hit her.

"Where are you hurt?" she asked. She hooked her hands in my armpits and brought my face up to the truck's headlights. "Can you walk?"

"Don't touch me," I said. "I hate you."

"Carenne," she said. "I'm sorry. Please. I have to get you home. Tell me if you can walk."

I couldn't stop crying. The blood running down my throat made the hiccups worse and I threw up again. Aleo scooped up some snow and wiped my mouth. My cheeks had numbed and I could see what she was doing without feeling it. "Spit that out," she said. "Come on. Spit it out." I kept my mouth closed and swallowed everything. I lay back on the ground and pressed my face against the snow. Aleo grabbed me and picked me up. It hurt and I told her to leave me alone. I yelled at her to never speak to me again. She carried me to the truck and shut the door. By that time my legs were aching. They felt like the skin had been ripped off and they were raw inside my jeans. I quit fighting and let her take me home.

Mom must have heard the screaming, because she was standing down by the mailbox with a flashlight. It caught the inside of the truck like a searchlight and Aleo threw up her hand to shield her eyes. She pulled in the drive and stopped the truck.

As soon as Mom saw me, she started screaming like a wild cat. "What happened? What is it?" She pulled the door open and reached for me. I covered my face with my hands and tried not to get sick again.

"Robin," I cried. "Robin." I tried to explain to Mom that I was crying because of Robin. Robin had gone away and Aleo didn't miss him the way I did. Aleo didn't miss him at all.

Mom put the flashlight to my face and pushed my hands away. She touched my cheek and I remembered then that I had spit up my teeth.

Aleo came around the other side of the truck. "It was an accident," she explained. "She fell out of the truck."

"Is she drunk?" Mom asked.

"We had a beer," Aleo said.

"She's fifteen," Mom screamed.

It was hard to hear what they were saying because of the roaring in my ear. I put my head back on the seat and closed my eyes to make the spinning stop. I remember they carried me inside. I couldn't get the words right to tell Mom that I wanted Robin home. All I could do was choke.

They put me on my bed and Mom put a warm cloth against my face. The skin was stinging and I kept crying.

"Do you think she should go to the hospital?" Aleo stood at

the end of my bed looking down at me. There was blood streaked across her jacket and for a moment I thought she had been hurt too. Then I realized that it was mine and she had carried me by herself. The room was a funny purple color, too dark around the edges. Mom came back with a new washcloth and her hand brushed against my leg. I started screaming. She tried to undo the zipper, but I wouldn't let her and finally she got a pair of scissors and cut straight through the material. The pillowcase stained quickly when I turned my face away and Mom asked Aleo to start up the truck to take me to the hospital. I tried one more time to tell Mom how awful it was that Robin was gone, but she told me to hush, to keep still and lie quiet.

I I I

Snow fell and the two months I spent in bed passed slowly. The wind drafted through the heavy plastic wrapped across the windows, facing the lake, sometimes blowing so hard the house would shake. At night I lay awake, tired of sleeping all day, and listened to the field mice in the walls. They made strange noises and I tried to imagine what they were building, what they were finding to eat. I would tap on the headboard and wait for the quick hush that would settle immediately. Dad came in to see me twice. The first time he walked right past the bed and dragged the dining room chair to the window. He sat down and started explaining the things he saw out there.

"Icicles off the shed," he said. "Going to bring down the roof if they get any heavier. Long white just won't stop."

"I can see it," I said. In Good Hart, winter is made up of only two colors, the white of the snow and the black of the trees. "Long white" is what the Finns call never-ending snow. Snow that doesn't stop for days.

"Lake froze this year," he said. "Ice is thick. Real thick out there."

"Come look at the scars on my leg," I told him. "You should see how long they are. Some of them go all the way down to my ankles." My knees had swollen up like summer melons and the cuts scabbed and drove me crazy with their itching. The skin on my legs looked like the bark of a birch tree and peeled just as easily. I lost two teeth and had a line of stitches in my right cheek, but I don't think Dad understood what I was doing in bed and ignored anything I said about the accident.

"Froze all the way to Wisconsin," Dad said. "You could walk across it if you had to."

"No one needs to walk to Wisconsin," I said. "They can drive there."

"Drive?" He said the word and shook his head.

"You can drive a car anywhere," I said. "Don't you know that, Dad?"

He stayed silent at the window. "Could fish," he said after a few moments. "Ice huts are built."

All I could see from the bed was the gray sky, day after day, which once in a while was interrupted by a string of birds cutting a straight line beneath the clouds. "Do you see any?" I asked.

"Don't have to," Dad said. "Ice huts are out there."

"Where?" I tried to make him talk.

"They're out there," he whispered. He ran his hands through his hair. Once the same color as Robin's blond, it was now gray. He looked worn out and his face was red as if he had recently been kissed by Superior's Demon.

I was tired of being by myself. My friends were in school all day and it was hard for them to come see me. Aleo didn't come to visit though I wished she would. I wanted desperately to talk with her. Every time I thought about the accident I felt horrible. Somehow even the fact that I couldn't walk and that I needed two new teeth didn't make up for the way I had acted. But there was another reason I wanted to talk to her. It was more than just to apologize. I wanted to see what more she might have to say about Dad.

He came in to see me the night before he disappeared. He sat down on the bed in silence and put something on top of the blankets. I liked it when he was around. He smelled of late fall, of old leaves, of something very pleasant that I associated with the time around his homecoming.

"Raha," he said. I recognized his leather wallet. Raha is Finnish for money, not just regular money, but saved money.

"What for?" I asked. I had been awake, sitting up in bed without the lights on, watching the clear white streaks of snow against the window.

"It's yours," he said.

"I can't spend money. I can't get out of bed," I said.

He patted the wallet and then took my hand and slipped it between my fingers.

"You keep it, Dad," I said. "I don't need it." I thought he wanted to tell me something, but he sat there quietly and we watched night until I fell asleep. In the morning he was gone and the wallet was hidden in the folds of the blanket. I counted out the money inside. There was over four hundred dollars. I hid the wallet between the mattress and the box spring for safekeeping and planned to give it back next time he wandered in.

I didn't tell Mom about the wallet right away and it took her a week to tell me Dad was gone. She started spending a lot of time in the chair next to my bed. She carried in the television and sat staring at the screen, her face serious even when a funny program was on. Some nights she'd fall asleep in the chair and begin to snore softly. The woman would sing the *Star Spangled Banner* and then static would hum through the night until the weather report came on in the morning. Mom used it as her alarm clock. She'd hear the deep voice of the broadcaster, and in a flash she'd be rushing to the kitchen to start the hot water for the oatmeal and coffee.

I didn't even guess that Dad wasn't in the house until finally it hit me that it had been days since I had heard him in the living room, moving from the couch to the refrigerator. I pictured him sitting out back, the steps piled high with snow, trying to see what he could of the lake. When I asked Mom what he was doing, she brushed the question aside.

"Did he go hunting?" I asked.

"No," she said.

"Is there something wrong with Dad?" I asked.

"Of course not," Mom said. She was busy with her sewing. I watched her bring the material up to her mouth and bite down on the loose threads.

"Then why does he act so strange all the time?" I sat up and flipped the pillow over. My back ached from sitting such a long time and, no matter how much I moved around, I still hurt all over.

"Dad's not interested in things on the land," she explained. "He's a water person. He's better off on the lakes."

"Did he go back on the ships?" I asked.

"Maybe," she said.

"You don't know?" I put my hand under the mattress and felt the soft leather of the wallet.

Mom could be mysterious when she wanted and her answer was vague.

"Well, when's he coming home?" I persisted.

"One of these days," she said.

"Soon?" I asked.

"I don't know," she admitted. She folded her dark material into a large awkward square and put it on top of the sewing basket. "How about a tuna sandwich for lunch?"

"You don't know when Dad's coming home?" I said.

"I'm sure it will be soon." She got up and brushed the tiny white threads from her skirt.

"Where'd he go?" I asked.

Mom had enough of my questions and walked out of the room. She came back with the tray with two sandwiches and a glass of milk. I reached under the mattress for the wallet and pulled it out when she set the tray on the bedside table.

"Dad gave me this," I said. Her eyes were wide when she saw the wallet and she looked at me in surprise.

"No." She shook her head firmly. "When did he give it to you?"

"I don't know," I said. "Last time he was in here."

"Was it Wednesday?" she asked. She picked up the wallet and turned it over as if looking for something specific.

"I can't remember," I said. I thought back to what I had been watching on television the night he came in. It was the only way I could keep track of the days.

She opened the wallet and the money spilled onto the covers.

"Oh no," she said. She scooped the bills together, some of them falling to the floor, and I saw that she was crying.

"What is it, Mom?" I asked. "What's wrong?"

"It's his raha," she said. She let the money go and left the room. I gathered the bills together and stacked them in a neat pile on the blanket. I heard the birdlike whistle of the phone dialing and held my breath as I strained to hear who Mom was calling. Her voice muffled through the walls and I knew she was deliberately talking in a low tone so I wouldn't hear.

"What is it?" I yelled when I could no longer hear the rumble of her voice. "Where's Dad?"

Mom appeared in the door frame. Her face was calm and she had stopped crying.

"I'm going out," she said. "If I can get the truck started, that is."

"Didn't Dad take the truck?" I asked.

"Of course not," Mom said. "It's right in the driveway."

"Where is he?" I asked again.

"I'm sure he went to visit some of his friends from the ship," she said. She moved the bucket I used for a toilet close to the bed where I could reach it. "Are you going to be all right alone?"

"Did Dad say anything about going to see someone?" The wind caught the large piece of plastic taped around my window like a sail. It billowed, holding taut for a moment, and then the bottom blew loose. We both turned to look.

"I won't be long," Mom said. "Try and get some rest." Her winter boots were old and the fur was dirty. The zipper on one was broken from too much use and she had to wrap masking tape around her calf to keep the snow out. I gave her the stack of money and Dad's wallet. She kissed me on my forehead and left the house.

After an hour of waiting for the sound of the truck in the driveway, I threw back the covers for another inspection of my knees. The scabs had almost all peeled off and the new skin was pink and very sore when I touched it. I swung my legs to one side of the bed and set my feet on the cold floor. I was dizzy when I first stood up, but my knees took the weight. They ached as I walked around the other side of the bed. I had to use the wall for support, but made it to the dresser until a stiffness in my knees told me that they couldn't take the pressure much longer. I saw myself in the mirror for the first time since the accident and was surprised at how little I had changed. My face was swollen, but the scar where the stitches had been wasn't noticeable. My hair, washed once a week, was pulled back in a tight ponytail and looked wet. It took me twice as long to make it back to bed and I was exhausted.

It was dark out when Mom got home. She carried a big bag of fried chicken from the takeout place in Pelston. The chicken was wrapped in tinfoil with Styrofoam containers of coleslaw and little packets of ketchup. Mom hates to eat out and I was surprised by her choice of dinner. I waited until we had finished all six chicken wings before asking about Dad.

"He's fine," she said. "I talked to Ed's wife. He's on the ship with Dad and she told me they all went up hunting muskrat in the Upper Peninsula."

"Why didn't he tell you about it?" I asked. Mom was very calm and it was easy to believe what she was telling me.

"You know Dad," she said. "He knows how upset I was about your accident. I'm sure he just didn't want to bother me."

I sipped at my Coke, trying to make it last.

"Dad's a very quiet man," Mom added. "He's not like everyone else. No. Not like anybody else around." She got her sewing out and we settled down to watch our television programs. I must have fallen asleep first because the television was off when I woke up in the morning and Mom was just getting up from her chair. The wind was very strong and, sometime during the night, the plastic covering around my window had blown away.

Robin called on Christmas Day and told us things weren't going as well as the Kingbees wanted in Los Angeles. He said they were heading back for a two-week gig in Duluth. The band wasn't sure where they were going after that, but he would call and let us know. I told him about my knee exercises, that I had started to walk around the house on crutches, and that Dad was still hunting muskrat in the Upper Peninsula. Mom told him to write her a postcard from Duluth. Things seemed back on track and I made plans to start school after the New Year.

The first day back at school came after a weekend storm. I thought for sure the roads would be blocked, but late Sunday night I heard the rumble of the snowplows coming down M119, and the next morning the air was filled with bright sunshine. The schoolrooms got hot with the fresh sun pouring in and everyone was restless from so much vacation. The teachers gave us an unexpected outdoor recess. A small group of senior and junior girls sat on the front steps with our faces turned to the sun. Laura Persley unwrapped her bologna sandwich and used the foil as a reflector to catch the sun. A few of the twelfth grade guys came over to bug us and for some reason they started in on me.

"Big year for you, isn't it, Conaway?" Todd Turnquist teased me.

"Did you jump out of that truck or did that crazy Indian push you?" someone else asked.

I kept my eyes shut and the sun made a chain of yellow dots in front of my eyes. Laura told them to get lost, but they ignored her.

"And now it's your dad," Todd said. "I'm surprised you're not cracking up."

"What do you know about my dad?" I asked. I opened my eyes to find everyone in the small group staring. Todd was standing over me, his body making a long shadow on the brick wall of the school building. "What did you say about my dad?"

"Don't listen to him," Laura told me. "He doesn't know what he's talking about."

"I'm only saying what everyone else in town can't stop talking about," Todd said. He held a cigarette between his lips and blew the smoke from his mouth without touching the cigarette. "Can't tell me that's not true."

"My dad's hunting muskrat in the UP," I told Todd. "I don't know what kind of stories you heard, but that's where he is."

"That accident must have affected your brain, not your knees, Conaway," Todd said. "There's no muskrat in the Upper Peninsula. Not this time of the year."

"Leave her alone." Laura crunched her tinfoil into a ball and whipped it at Todd. She came over and gave me a hand to help me stand up. A warning bell rang when we passed through the school doors.

"Are people saying things?" I asked Laura once we were alone inside. Laura was a grade ahead of me and had never been a good friend. But I knew she had had a crush on Robin when he was a senior and she sometimes paid me special attention.

"Not really," she said. She offered me half of the unwrapped sandwich. I took it, but didn't eat.

"Nothing?" I asked. "You sure about that?"

"A few rumors are flying around," she said. "But no one's talking about it."

"Tell me," I said.

"A lot of people think your dad's not quite right," she said. "You know what I mean?"

"What are they saying about him?" My hands were sweating and the bologna sandwich was getting soft. I tossed it over to the garbage can and missed. It opened in two, the bright yellow mustard smearing on the side of the can.

"I don't know how it started, but someone said your dad went into the General Store up in Cross Village and told Lola he was going to jump off the Mackinac Bridge."

"What?" I took a sharp breath and the sides of my mouth were instantly dry. "What?"

"You know how things get passed around town," she said. "I'm sure he just said he felt like jumping off a bridge. The winters make everyone batty."

"It's not true," I said. "Honest. It's just not true."

Laura told me I didn't look so good and she led me over to my desk by the window. My knees were stiff and they protested when I tried to make them bend. The sun had moved behind a large cloud and we stood in the afternoon shadows of a short January day.

"Of course it's not true," Laura said. "It's just a story. I don't even know how Todd Turnquist found out about it."

"Does anyone else know?"

"No," Laura said firmly. "No one knows a thing."

"Really?" I pressed her. "Really?"

Some of the kids started coming into the classroom and Laura gave me a big smile. "Don't be upset," she said. "It's nothing." She went back to her own classroom, one floor up.

But by the time school got out at three-thirty I knew everyone was talking about it. I only had to look around the room to see that people weren't staring at me because of the truck accident, but because they had heard a story about Dad. I tried not to pay attention to their looks, but the ringing in my ears roared louder and louder. I watched the clock tick off the seconds until the final bell rang and then I got up slowly and walked toward the girls' locker room down at the opposite end of school, far away from the kids waiting for the buses. Laura came up to me and asked if anything was wrong.

"No," I said. "I'm fine. I have to stay after school to catch up on some math homework."

"You going to miss the bus?" she asked.

"Mom's coming to get me," I lied. "She knows I have to stay after."

"When's Robin coming back to town?" Laura asked.

"One of these days," I said. My knees hurt from standing too long, but I tried not to show how I felt. "Soon."

"I can't wait to hear the Kingbees sing," she said.

"I'll tell Robin you said hello."

Laura pulled on her hat, the same blue as her mittens, and her blonde hair disappeared.

"Thanks, Laura," I said. "See you."

The girls' locker room is right next to the pool and the smell of chlorine bit into my nose and stung my eyes. I cried into my hands, trying to keep quiet in case someone walked in. The junior basketball team started practicing in the gym. The balls bouncing on the wooden floor vibrated the lockers, and I knew no one could hear me. I waited forty-five minutes, giving even the bus from Levertown time to load up and drive off. I got up and washed my face and cut across the snowy parking lot to the highway and stuck out my thumb.

The first car that drove by stopped for me. I recognized the guy. He had been a few years ahead of Robin in school and he worked construction. I had also seen him working at the lumber store in Pelston. His car was filled with painting supplies and he had to move some stuff around so I could fit in the front seat.

"Miss the school bus?" he asked after I got in and closed the door.

"Yeah," I said. The car stalled and he started it up again. It flooded and we waited a minute before he got it going.

"Where you headed?" he asked.

"I need a ride to Indiantown," I said.

"Indiantown?" He looked over at me real surprised and I knew he was checking out the color of my cheeks. There was paint on his hands and his nails were stained the same yellow color. "Why you going up there?"

"It's important," I said. "I got to go up and see my brother's girlfriend."

"Indiantown?" he repeated. "I'm not even sure where that is."

"Maybe you know my brother," I explained. We were heading in the right direction and I knew he would take me where I needed to go. "He plays for the Kingbees."

"What are you? Robin's sister?" he said.

"Yeah," I said. It felt good to be sitting in the warm car. I relaxed and let him tell me all the things he knew about Robin and the Kingbees.

"Great band," he said. "Where are they now?"

"They're on their way home from California," I said. "I want to go and meet them at the bridge."

He got quiet and turned up the radio. I wondered if he had heard something about Dad. We were one of the few cars on the road and he drove fast. The Pelston airport was closed because of the heavy snow over the weekend and the runway looked strange without the red lights. The guy knew the turn-off and followed my directions to the line of low shedlike buildings. The small sign in the one window was still flashing. I offered to give the guy some money for driving me so far out of his way, but he wouldn't take any. "Be careful," he warned.

My legs had cramped and it took a few extra minutes to get out of the car. I thought about asking him to wait while I went in, but couldn't get the words right. I felt strange just walking in the bar so I knocked on the door and waited. There was some noise coming from inside, and I wasn't sure if anyone had heard my knock. I tried again. An old man opened the door. His large frame blocked the way and I couldn't see past him into the bar.

"I'm looking for Aleo," I told him. "Is she here?"

I heard her call my name from the back of the room and the old man moved to one side so I could go in, but for some reason my legs wouldn't move right. I didn't know if it was from sitting so long cramped in the car or if it was because I was afraid.

"Carenne," Aleo called my name again. "Shut the door and get in here."

But for some reason I couldn't walk.

She called to me again. "Hurry up. The wind is horrible."

I was paralyzed. "I can't," I yelled to her. I looked down at my legs and my blue jeans looked like they always did, but I couldn't make them walk into the bar.

She came over and took me by the arm to a chair just inside the door. Her grip was strong. "What is it?" she asked. "What are you doing up here?"

"I have to find the Kingbees, Aleo," I said. "Something's really wrong. I've got to find Robin."

Aleo shook her head. The old man who had opened the door stood next to us. Aleo shooed him away and he moved across the room, slowly dragging his feet.

"Do you know where the Kingbees are?" I asked. "I've got to find them."

Words started coming out of my mouth and I couldn't stop them. "I'm sorry about what happened that night," I told Aleo. "It was all my fault. You were right. Something's happened to Dad. Mom won't tell me anything. I have to talk to Robin." I stopped to catch my breath and Aleo put her finger to her lips.

"Shush," she said. "It's okay." Her voice was much lower

than mine and I realized I must have been shouting. "Are your knees okay?"

"Do you know where the Kingbees are?" I whispered. "You don't understand how important it is."

"Does your mom know you came here?" she asked.

I felt like I was going to pass out, so I put my head between my legs and took some deep breaths. The floor smelled like stale beer and old leather. Aleo pulled up a chair next to me and waited. "Of course she has no idea you're here," she said. "I'm going to call her."

"It doesn't matter," I said. "I have to find the Kingbees."

Aleo pushed the hair off her face and in a quick twist knotted it up into a ponytail.

"I shouldn't be the one to tell you this," Aleo said. "But the Kingbees are still in California."

"No," I said. "Robin called at Christmas and said they were leaving."

"The band's still there," she said.

At first I thought there might be something wrong between Aleo and Robin and that maybe Robin had lied to her about where he was.

"He was on his way to Duluth," I said. "They have a two-week gig there."

"Robin left without the band," Aleo said.

"What are you talking about?" I put my head against the back of the chair and tried to get everything straight. The bar looked just as I had remembered. It even seemed as if the same people were there. The windowsill was dusty and the flashing sign made a small pool of light on the floor.

"I'm going to call your mom." Aleo stood up. "She's probably going crazy with worry over you."

"Tell me where Robin is first," I said. "I have to know."

"You stay here," Aleo said.

She went behind the partition on the other side of the room and the old man came over with a glass of Coke. There wasn't any ice and the drink was flat. I set it on the table without finishing it.

Aleo came back and told me to come away from the door, away from the draft. I followed her to a table and she motioned for me to take my coat off.

"Why isn't Robin in Duluth?" I asked.

"He was," she said. "But he's gone on."

"Without the band?"

"Yes," Aleo said.

"Why?" I asked. "I don't get it."

"Your mom thought she was protecting you," Aleo said. "She didn't want to make you upset."

"Did Dad jump off the Mackinac Bridge?"

"What?" An evening shadow fell across half of her face. "Where did you hear that?"

"At school," I said. "Todd Turnquist told me that everyone in town knows Dad jumped off the bridge."

"Well, it's news to me," Aleo said. "But that's why Robin had to leave the band for a while."

"To find Dad?" I asked.

Aleo nodded.

"Mom doesn't know where he is?" I put my hands together and rubbed them back and forth. They were dry from the cold air. "He didn't go hunting?"

"No," Aleo said. "No one knows where he is."

"Oh no," I said. I could feel the tears in the back of my throat start to rise to my eyes, but I was getting so tired from crying. I wanted to keep my head clear. "Where is he?"

"I don't know," Aleo said. "He just seemed to vanish."

The snow flew around the windowpanes in quick jerky movements. The wind carried it vertically across the parking lot in bursts of energy which reminded me of waves—the sudden blast of snow hurling at the window and then a sudden stillness.

"Why didn't Mom tell me?" I asked. "She should have told me."

Aleo got up and came back with two cups of coffee. "Drink up," she said. "It will calm you down."

I didn't say anything for a while. The image of Dad walking down a deserted road stayed in my mind until I thought of the summer—the long months that Dad was on the ships. I could see him clearly in my mind. His gray hair tousled without Mom's comb and his face deep red from the lake. I imagined him walking on the ship's deck, his arms on the shoulders of the person in front of him, and I knew that Dad was not alone.

"He's not around here," I said suddenly. Aleo watched me closely. She told me to calm down and drink the coffee. It wasn't as bitter or as hot as I had expected. I sipped it and the warm drink made things clearer in my head.

"Did he tell you anything?" she asked. "The night he left— did he say anything to you about where he might go?"

"He's with the Demon." I spoke confidently. "That's where he would go. He's near Superior."

Aleo came around the table and sat on the floor in front of me. She took my hands and began to rub them with her own. Her skin was smooth and after a moment a numb feeling took over below my wrists.

"Did he say that?" she asked softly. I pulled my hand away to drink more of the sweet coffee.

"No," I said. "But that's where he is. I know it."

Aleo's voice was as smooth as the approaching darkness. "That's what Robin thinks too."

"I want to see Robin," I said. "Do you know where he is?"

"He called me last night from Marquette," Aleo said. "He's been traveling around the towns on Lake Superior trying to find your dad."

"So there wasn't any gig in Duluth?" I asked. It seemed to all be making sense now—Robin's hesitation to talk about my accident and how little he had talked about the band. He had never even asked me once about Dad.

Aleo got up off the floor without answering. Her jeans were

worn at the knees—red socks showed through the criss-crossed threads.

"Can you take me up to Marquette?" I asked. "I'm going to help Robin find Dad."

Aleo nodded slightly. It seemed to me that she was moving awfully slowly. I had to get her to hurry and take me to see Robin so I stood and picked up my knapsack.

"I have to go up there," I said.

"I can't take you," she said. "The truck's dead." She nodded toward the back of the room as if it was parked right there and I could see that it wouldn't start up.

I stomped my feet and started yelling at her. "You don't care about Dad," I yelled. "You think he's crazy."

She was watching me in surprise, but she didn't make a move.

"Dad talks to me," I yelled. "I can find him. I know I can. I have to." I was really screaming at her and my throat was getting raw. The other people in the bar were staring. The two guys had quit playing pool, but I didn't care.

"I don't think he's crazy. You know that's not true," Aleo said. She moved her hands to quiet me, but I got out of her way. "All right. All right. We'll do something."

I followed her to the back of the bar and she started making phone calls. The guy at the bus stop in Mackinac City said the Greyhound had just left. It was crossing over the Mackinac Bridge and would stop for a forty-five-minute dinner break in St. Ignace. He promised to call ahead and warn the driver that we were trying to catch it. Aleo borrowed a green station wagon and we left right away. All the way up, I kept praying for Aleo to drive faster.

IV

But it didn't happen at all like I thought it would. Not at all like I wanted it to.

Aleo must have called Robin, because he was standing in the doorway of the Porcupine Bar when we pulled into Marquette. A dark shadow covered most of his body and at first I didn't recognize him. His hair was blond at the roots and the dark ends looked as if they had been dipped in black paint. He saw me through the window and got on the bus to help me off.

"Do you need me to carry you?" he asked. "Mom said you were still having problems getting around."

"I'm fine," I said. "Almost as good as new."

He bent over and lifted me off the seat. I had to reach down to grab my knapsack. The other passengers were all awake and they stared at us. The driver told us to have a good night.

"I can walk," I protested, but Robin carried me outside. The aisle was narrow and dark and I had been fighting off sleep for the last two hours. I was just as glad not to walk.

"We're going to find Dad," I whispered in his ear. "I'm sure of it."

Robin put me down on the snowbank and opened the car door. I got up slowly and walked over. "You shouldn't have come up here," he said. "Not with your knees all bad and everything."

"Why not?" I said. "You left the Kingbees."

"It's not the same thing," Robin said.

"I really think I can help," I told him. "I know just where Dad is. Can't you see him, sitting around watching the waves on the shore of Superior?"

"The lake is frozen," Robin said.

"Not Superior," I said. "Dad says it's too deep to freeze."

"People around here say it froze." Robin let the car run a moment and the heater started up slowly.

"Then those people are morons," I said. "Dad knows more about this lake than all of them put together."

"Aleo told me you were getting stubborn." The car was having problems getting traction on the ice and we slid sideways a couple of feet.

"What else did she say?" I asked. I was going to tell Robin

that Aleo had called Dad crazy, but knew it wasn't the right time.

Robin got the car in control and we pulled slowly out onto the main road. The plows had pushed the snow to the side of the streets and at some parts the banks were higher than the car.

"Where you staying up here?" I asked. "Do you know they have a hotel here that looks like a ship?"

"I haven't seen it," Robin said.

"Dad says the windows on the top floor are shaped like portholes and you can see the bay from there."

Robin started speaking real soft and I thought he was going to give me a lecture about leaving town without telling Mom, so I said I was starving. The bus had stopped in Escanaba, but I didn't have change for the vending machines. Robin pointed to the back seat and I found a shopping bag full of store-bought sandwiches and potato chips.

"Anything to drink back here?"

"Listen, Carenne," he said. "We're not staying in Marquette tonight."

"Why not?" I asked. "You haven't looked for him here. I know I can find him. He's always talking about this area. He loves it."

"Wait. Wait," Robin said. "You've got to slow down and let me talk. It seems like a lot of things are changing now."

I wanted to let him talk, but I had been thinking so much about my plan to find Dad that I just couldn't let him. I wanted to tell him that I could find Dad if he would just let me.

"We're going to Sault Ste. Marie," Robin said firmly.

I turned around and saw the lights of the city lining the large bay. We were driving away from it.

"The Soo?" I asked. "Why? Shouldn't we look here first?"

"I thought so too," Robin said. "That's what I thought too." I had never seen him cry before and I was so shocked that I started crying too.

"Please don't be upset with me," I said. I dropped the potato chip bag on the floor and smeared the salt on the car seat. "I'm sorry. I don't want to be stubborn."

"It's not you," Robin said. He was crying so hard that he had to pull over to the shoulder. He cried deep in his throat and it hurt me to hear him. He stopped the car and got out. It was dead cold and the night was pitch black. I wasn't sure what to do so I sat and waited. I blew on my hands to keep them warm.

"Did Dad jump off the Mackinac Bridge?" I asked him when he got back in.

"Is that what they're saying in Good Hart?" he asked. We drove down the highway, away from the lights of Marquette.

"Someone at school told me that," I said.

"I don't know what happened," Robin said. "He's just gone. Like he just disappeared."

"He didn't say anything to Mom?"

"Nothing," Robin said. "I don't know what he was thinking when he took off."

"Please, can't we look for him here?" The driving was making my legs shake and they hurt so much I was starting to lose feeling in them.

"We have to go to Sault Ste. Marie," Robin said.

"I don't get it," I said. "Why should we go there when we might have to come back here?"

"There's a man down there who thinks he saw Dad," Robin said. "He thinks he saw Dad a couple of months ago."

"How do you know that? Who told you that?"

"The police have been asking questions," Robin said.

"The police? Does Mom know the police are looking for him?"

"She's the one who called them," Robin said. A light snow started to fall out of the darkness, heading straight for the headlights. Robin turned on the windshield wipers.

"Do you think something bad happened?" I asked. "What did the man say?"

"I'm not sure," Robin said.

"Let me help look for him," I begged. "Please. I know I can find him."

Robin cleared his throat and sat forward to rub the windshield, but it didn't help. The snow was coming down faster than the wipers could keep it off.

It took us twice as long to get to the Soo because of the storm. We tried to stop along the way, but none of the motels on the highway were open. Robin said we would freeze to death if we tried sleeping on the side of the road. So I made him sing to me—every single song the Kingbees do and then some from the radio. At first he wouldn't, but I think he changed his mind because he was afraid of falling asleep at the wheel. I kept my eyes on the road and stayed up the whole way there.

Sault Ste. Marie was gray and quiet when we pulled in. We drove straight to a motel near the locks. The guy at the desk told us Mom had been calling almost every hour. She was frantic with worry. We had traveled right in the center of the storm. The radio was reporting drifting up to three feet. We went up to the room and Robin called Mom to tell her we were all right.

The bathroom had a shelf of folded white towels. I started filling the tub with hot water and listened to Robin on the phone. After he hung up, he yelled through the closed door that Mom was coming. Someone from Good Hart was giving her a ride. The phone rang again. I couldn't hear what Robin was saying, so I turned off the water and opened the door an inch. He was standing in front of the mirror brushing back his hair with his fingers.

"Was that Mom again?"

"I want you to get some sleep," Robin said. "You've been sick in bed for months and I don't want you to get worse up here."

"I jumped out of a truck, Robin," I said. "I haven't been sick a day this year. Tell me who was on the phone."

Robin came into the bathroom and wet his face. He threw the towel on the floor and I went over and picked it up.

"Tell me," I said.

"It was the guy who contacted the police, the one who thinks he saw Dad. He wants me to meet him across the street."

"I'm coming too," I said.

"I'd rather you didn't," Robin said.

"Why not?"

"Because. I think it would be better if you stayed here."

"If it's about Dad then I want to hear it too," I said. "How are we ever going to find him if we don't start looking?"

"Okay. Get your coat on," Robin said. He went over to the dresser, where he had emptied his pockets. He tucked his wallet inside his jacket and scooped the change into the ashtray. I waited for him at the door and just before we left the room, he turned to me and said, "You should know that what this guy has to tell us probably won't be good news."

"If it's about Dad, it's got to be good news," I said. My mittens were wet in my coat pocket. I put them on and then took them off again.

"I sure hope so," Robin said.

The bar was already half filled at ten o'clock in the morning. There was a large window looking out over Superior and the gray water seemed to take over the room. The locks were quiet. I stared up at the tower, but couldn't see anyone moving around inside. A waitress came over and we ordered coffee. Robin asked her if Jon Jarrenfelt was in the bar. She took a long look around and told us he wasn't there at the moment, but not to fret because it wouldn't be too long before he'd be in.

"Nothing else for the guys to do this time of year. Just keep

on coming in and out of this place," she told us. "I swear when
the snow falls heavy like this, the whole crew of them start
acting like boomerangs."

I poured three packs of powdered cream in my coffee. She
didn't give us any spoons so I stirred it with the handle of my
fork. We both kept watch on the door. A little while later an
old man walked in and headed straight for our table. Robin
stood up and shook his hand.

"Got to be you two," the old man said. "You're the only
strangers in town this time of year."

Even before he sat down, the waitress brought him coffee in
a glass and beside it set a shot glass filled to the top with something amber-colored. He held it up to Robin and told him it
was winter's milk, changed color for warmth. Robin said he'd
have one too.

Mr. Jarrenfelt finished his shot and started sipping on his
coffee. "Not a year goes by that Superior doesn't remind us
she's in charge," he said. "People think they can tame her, but
she doesn't even let them come close."

Mr. Jarrenfelt was a Finn. I could tell by his eyebrows. He
had dark hair on his head, but his eyebrows were so white that
at first glance it looked like he didn't have any.

"Ten years ago people were forgetting about her power,"
Mr. Jarrenfelt went on. "She never let the ships alone in the
winter, but they thought they could control her. That's when
she sunk the *Edmund Fitzgerald*. Right out there."

I wanted him to hurry and start talking about Dad. I didn't
understand why Robin was so interested in listening to the old
guy tell stories about Sault Ste. Marie. I started to interrupt, but
Robin put his hand over mine and I went back to stirring the
cream into my coffee.

"Just a summer ago three kids were walking on the break
wall, middle of July. A storm broke across the water and she
swallowed them up." Mr. Jarrenfelt drank the coffee as fast as
he drank the shot. Robin offered to get him another. "They
were only two miles out. Still in sight of shore and the Demon

wouldn't let go of those kids' bodies. Families couldn't do anything about it. They ended up burying clothes. Caskets without
bodies. That's what you find in cemeteries around here."

The waitress came back over, carrying a tray with two more
shots of whiskey and the coffee pot.

"Did you see my Dad?" I asked when Mr. Jarrenfelt stopped
to thank the waitress. I knew Robin was angry, but I didn't care.
I couldn't wait any longer. Robin apologized to Mr. Jarrenfelt.
He said we were both anxious to find Dad and that's why I was
being rude.

Mr. Jarrenfelt finished the shot and then wiped his mouth
with the back of his hand. "It's okay. I was just coming around
to the story," he said. "See, I live out of town a ways. Just west
of here, on the shore. Couple of months ago I was out shovel-
ing the drive and I saw someone walking out on the ice. At
first I thought I was seeing things. Snow blindness or
something."

"Could you see his face?" Robin asked.

"It was the man the police had the photograph of," Mr. Jarrenfelt said. "Clear fact. Sure as I'm sitting here."

"Are you positive?" Robin played with the shot glass before
taking a drink. Then he finished it all at once.

"Just like I told you. We don't see that many new folks
around here in the winter months, so when I saw someone
wandering around practically in my own backyard, I paid him
some attention."

"What happened to him?" I asked. I pushed the coffee to
one side and sat forward in my chair.

"Well, that's the story," Mr. Jarrenfelt said. "The man just kept
on walking along the shore and I called to him to tell him to
be careful. I know he heard me. The wind'll carry your voice
to Grand Marais if you want it to."

"What did he do?" Robin asked.

"Just kept walking. He turned around once and looked at
me, but then started walking, this time away from shore."

"Going into the lake?" I asked.

Mr. Jarrenfelt nodded. "I kept my eye on him for a quarter of an hour, but the wind was kicking up the snow so bad, I just lost sight of him." He coughed when he finished his second shot. He pounded on his chest with his fist, but it seemed to make it worse.

"I guess he got swallowed up by the Demon." Jarrenfelt kept coughing.

"Is there a chance he was walking toward something?" Robin asked. "Like a ship, or a boat, something docked away from shore?"

"No question that he was walking toward something," Mr. Jarrenfelt said. "No question in my mind."

"Where did he go?" I asked.

"He was walking into the arms of the most powerful woman in the world."

Robin was staring out the window and I had to inch my chair over to see what he was looking at. The low clouds were moving out over the lake and at the horizon they looked as if they touched.

"Is there any chance he could have made it across to the other shore?"

"Superior won't let you walk across her," Mr. Jarrenfelt said.

Robin hit his fist on the table. "I heard talk over in Marquette that the lake froze this year," he said. "Is there any chance my dad could have heard the same thing and thought he could walk across to Canada?"

"I think the Canadian fur smugglers get those rumors started," Mr. Jarrenfelt said. "You know, so that people think they're coming across the lake, when they're really just driving across the bridge like everybody else. Anyone who knows anything about the lake knows she's too deep to freeze."

Robin got up and went to the window. He stretched his arms overhead and moved his head as if he was watching something out there. I couldn't look at anything anymore—the light in the room was beginning to sting my eyes—so I stared at the damp wood floor where the snow from our boots was melting.

Robin came back to the table, but didn't sit down. "Your guess is that he walked into Superior?"

Mr. Jarrenfelt stood up and put his arm around Robin's shoulder. "I don't know what your dad was doing out there," he said. "Maybe she called to him and he couldn't resist. What I'm telling you is the truth. I saw him walk away from shore and disappear into the lake. I'm not sure if he fell into a crack in the ice or if Superior just reached out and brought him down to her. I just don't know."

I put my face on the table and wrapped my arms around my head so no one would hear me crying. I didn't want to listen to Mr. Jarrenfelt anymore. It all sounded so much like Dad, as if Dad himself was telling me what had happened. Robin came over and whispered in my ear that we were going back to the motel. He let me cry a few more minutes and then put his hand in mine and we walked out together. I didn't look at anyone, but kept my eyes on the floor and let Robin lead me across the street.

When we got back in the room, I had stopped crying and was getting angry.

"Do you believe the story?" I asked Robin. "Do you think Dad really walked into Superior?"

Robin went over and closed the curtains. He sat down on the bed and started untying his bootlaces without answering my questions.

"I'm sorry, Carenne," he said. "I wish you didn't have to be in this situation." Robin pulled the extra blanket from the closet and got one of the pillows to make a bed for himself on the floor. "But I think we should try and make this easier for Mom," he said. "You're going to have to be as strong as you can."

"Then you believe the story?" I sat down on the edge of the bed. Robin was on the floor with his face into the pillow. He was quiet and then he turned over and saw me watching him.

"Do you think Dad's dead?" I asked.

"I heard the same story you did."

I was afraid to tell Robin what Dad had told me about being at the bottom of Superior with the Demon, because saying it would make it that much closer to the truth. I twisted the bedspread in my hand and tried not to start crying again. Robin told me I should get some sleep and I said I was afraid of dreaming about Dad. Robin didn't say anything and after a while I must have gone to sleep because when I woke up I heard him crying. I felt too sad and horrible to say anything so I lay there with my eyes closed, listening to him. The second time I woke up, Robin was in the shower. I could tell by the long shadows falling across the bedspread that it was late afternoon. I turned on the television and watched the program until he came out. The room filled up quickly with warm air and the smell of soap.

"Do you want to shower or anything?" he asked. "Mom should be here soon."

"I can't take a shower," I said. "The water hurts my legs."

"Wash up, then," he said. "I'll go down to the desk and watch out for Mom."

"I don't want to be alone," I said. "I'm afraid to be here alone."

Robin came over and hugged me. He didn't tell me not to be afraid and I knew he was just as scared as I was. "Hurry up," he said. "I'll wait for you."

Mom was in a temper when she got to the hotel. Robin and I had been sitting in the lobby drinking Cokes and playing pinball. Robin smoked half a pack of cigarettes and I ate about four candy bars. Mom refused to go in the bar. She wanted Jarrenfelt to show us the place where he thought he saw Dad. Robin said he couldn't ask him to take us out there, but Mom wouldn't have it any other way.

"How else am I going to know if this old man is telling the truth?" she asked. Robin went across the street to get Jarrenfelt and Mom and I waited out by the car. My boots were still damp from the long ride to the Soo and I moved around, trying to keep my toes warm.

"The winter sure makes this place look sad," Mom said. "I don't like it one bit."

I knew what she meant. In the summer the red-bellied ships passing through the locks keep the place alive with people and noise. The guys on board hang over the sides and scream out to their friends and family. The ship moves slowly into the holding area. It rests even with the dock for a long time and then the water drains from that area and the ship lowers to Lake Michigan's level—fifteen feet below the dock. The people on the shore move down to the break wall to see the ship start out, as it heads south to Chicago.

Jarrenfelt offered to take us in his truck. He said we could all fit, but Mom didn't want to do that. I ended up riding with Jarrenfelt and Mom and Robin followed behind. Jarrenfelt didn't stop talking all the way to his house. He went on and on about everything that had happened in the Soo and this time I didn't interrupt.

Evening was close by when we started walking across the snowdrifts near Superior. The wind came at us as strong as I've ever felt it and as much as I tried to keep my head up, the cold stung so bad that I had to keep looking at my boots. Mom walked right out. I don't think she was paying any attention to the wind or the cold.

"How was he walking?" Mom asked.

"Right along here," Jarrenfelt called. "Straight out to the lake."

"No. I mean, was he walking fast or slow? Did it look like someone was chasing him?"

"Wasn't a soul out here except us."

Mom kept walking forward and we tried to keep up. The ice was thick beneath our feet and it didn't seem like it could ever melt. The sun felt miles away. At one point Jarrenfelt held back and refused to walk any further.

"She spooks me," he said. "Could all be superstition, but I'm not taking any chances. Some folks say there's a crack in the lake. Whole ships have been known to disappear."

We were about a mile from shore when Mom suddenly turned around and stood firm. The ice shifted and the sharp sound echoed around us. The noise seemed to scare Mom because she grabbed hold of Robin's arm and he held her steady. "I don't believe it. Not one word," she said. "It's just not true. I know it. Dad hates winter. He never would have walked out here."

"Ma, Jarrenfelt says the guy was wearing a long gray coat with black earmuffs—just like Dad's," Robin said.

"I say we're wasting time," Mom said. "Dad can't stand ice and cold wind."

"I don't think this guy's making up the story, Mom." Robin was looking down at his boots and his scarf was wrapped around his face up to his eyes.

"You believe everything strangers tell you?"

"Why would he go to all the trouble to contact the police if it wasn't true?"

"I can't explain human nature to you," Mom said. "He's a Finn raised in the UP. How would I know why he does what he does?"

The light was fading and it was getting harder to see our breath. Far beneath us, the ice cracked. It was a loud noise, muffled by the layers of snow.

"You're not making any sense," Robin said. "He didn't make it up. He saw someone walking on the beach."

Mom grabbed my hand and turned back to shore.

Robin stood where he was. "Then you tell me where Dad is," he called after us. "Where the hell is he?" The wind blowing toward the lake caught his words and soon we couldn't hear him anymore.

But I knew she was wrong. Mom was wrong. I broke away

from her and started running back to Robin. The wind drifted the snow in different layers. At some parts, it was up to my calves and then all of a sudden there would be a stretch of bare ice. I had a hard time keeping my balance. As I got closer, I could hear Robin calling for Dad. His voice was smooth and loud just like when he sings. The air held onto his voice for a while and then it let go and the sound just dropped down into the ice and disappeared.

"He can't hear you," I said. "He's at the bottom."

"I know," Robin said.

"He's with the Demon," I said. "That's where he told me he'd be."

We couldn't see very far in front of us. The night had come from the north across Superior and it was hard to tell where the sky ended and where the snow on the lake took over. The wind died down and we stood there for a long time—just standing there, not seeing anything, just looking out into the dark.

"We'll come back in the summer," Robin said.

"I want to come back and say good-bye," I said.

Using the yellow lights on the shoreline as a guide, we found our way back to the truck. We left for Good Hart that night.

V

And right away, just as soon as we got back to town, she started bugging Robin to play at Gert's Gas Stop. Robin said, seeing all that had happened, he didn't think it was such a good time. Mom wouldn't listen to him. She went down and asked Gert if they could move things around inside the shop so Robin and the band could set up their equipment. Gert said she'd be glad to do anything to help. She was worried about the motor oil freezing, outside, but then someone else offered to store it in their heated garage while the Kingbees played. Robin kept refusing and Mom kept insisting.

She spent most of her time inside sitting on the couch. I think she was waiting for Dad to come walking through the door, his hair blown back and his face all red. Some days she'd talk about him for hours, showing me old photographs of when Robin and I were babies. Other days she wouldn't let me mention him. She made me promise that I wouldn't tell anyone anything if they asked me. I was to stick to the story that Dad was hunting. Kids at school asked me all the time what had happened to Dad and I tried to ignore them. I spent a lot of time away from school. Mom didn't care how many days I missed. I think she liked having me around the house with her. My legs got stronger and stronger and after a while the aching inside stopped completely.

Near the end of March Robin and Aleo came over and Robin said he'd been thinking about it a lot and he finally decided he would sing by himself at Gert's. The band wouldn't do it, but he said he could do all their songs. He would play outside.

"Outside?" Mom asked. I could tell she thought it was some kind of trick. "You can't play outside. There's still snow on the ground."

"We thought we should get things going now," Aleo said.

"We need time to advertise," Robin said.

"What do you mean advertise?" Mom got up off the couch and put on water for hot chocolate. Robin looked over at me and winked. I smiled back at him.

"We have to let people know what's going on," Robin followed Mom into the kitchen. "If it's going to be bigger than the Jurff Pancy story, we have to get people to come to it."

I went over and hugged Aleo. I had a feeling this was her idea.

"Thank you," I whispered.

"Your dad's not unhappy," she said. "That's where he wanted to be."

"Do you think he's happy with the Demon?" I asked.

"It's your mom that we have to worry about," Aleo said.

Mom brought in the hot chocolate. "I don't think you should waste money on advertising." She was arguing with Robin. "We can just tell everyone. Word gets around quick enough."

"The folks up in Indiantown think it's a great idea," Aleo said. She took the cup from Mom. "They want people to forget about Jurff Pancy just as much as you do."

"They gave us some money to advertise," Robin said. "They think we should make it as big as possible."

Mom told me to sit on the floor and sat in my chair. She was quiet for a moment. She seemed surprised that the Indians would agree with her. "That makes sense." She nodded. "I can see why they'd want people to stop talking about Jurff. I can see why they'd feel that way."

Robin wouldn't let Mom make the posters at the house like she wanted to. He had them done at a sign shop in Pelston. They were light blue with dark letters. There was a photograph of Robin and his guitar standing under the Gert's Gas sign in the center with the date right next to it. Mom and I drove all over northern Michigan with rolls of masking tape. We put the posters up everywhere—every telephone pole, every bare space of building we could find. Robin and Aleo made a radio advertisement that ran almost every two hours on the Pelston station.

The day he played was the first real warm day we've had this year. Spring only officially arrived a week before, but except for the bare trees and the clumps of dirty snow still hiding in the ditches, it looked like the middle of summer. Traffic on M119 was backed up for miles with people driving into town. A guy from a newspaper in Detroit even came up to take photographs of Robin. All the Kingbees were there and I bet they wished they had sung too. Robin gave me a piece of paper and I went through the crowds asking everyone what they wanted to hear. Robin sang them all. People just kept coming and once they got there they didn't leave. Not even when it got dark and the cold settled in. I've never seen Mom so happy.

He sang over a week ago and the whole town's still buzzing about it. So I guess Mom was right—you just have to give people something new to chew the fat about.

Robin and I have been talking and he thinks it's all right to say that Dad ran away with another woman. He said Dad considered Superior his woman—always calling to him, always chasing him. She was the kind of woman who wouldn't let him rest here in town, on land so far away from her. So that's what I'm going to tell anyone who asks. It's not really a big deal. Not like Jurff Pancy murdering his wife and St. Bernard or Robin playing in front of Gert's, because a man going away with a woman, someone who's not his wife, is nothing new up here in Good Hart.